The Monster Junkies

An American Family Odyssey

The Monster Junkies
An American Family Odyssey

A novel by Erik Daniel Shein
and L. M. Reker

ArkWatch™
Entertainment through Imagination

Arkwatch Holdings LLC
4766 east Eden Drive
Cave Creek, AZ 85331

1-800-682-4650
www.arkwatch.com

ISBN 978-0-615-25020-5

Cover design by Jera Publishing: www.jerapublishing.com

Arkwatch Holdings LLC is an intellectual property holding company founded in 2003 by Erik Daniel Shein. The company's objective is to be one of the world's leading producers and providers of entertainment and information

Mission

Arkwatch Holdings believes that the intellectual properties we create, distribute, license, and put out into the marketplace have an environmental message that will make the world a safer and better place

BOOK I

Being a Normal Family is Just a State of Mind

Authors Note:

I want to stress that this is a work of fiction and we have played with source myths and legends to fold them into a story that, while we hope is entertaining, also contains something in which we believe strongly and hope will resonate with all who read this book. We need to cherish and protect our world's living treasures—animals and plant life. We have lost so many and so much through ignorance, which is understandable, *to a degree*, and greed, which is unconscionable. We must do better and eliminate both.

We all were all MonsterJunkies and wear masks during our daily lives, in school, during work, hanging out with our friends, imitating, being people who we look up to and admire, or those we want to be. It is the people who take off their masks and show the real person inside who are the ones that truly find meaning in their lives.

Who are the real monsters? People who wear masks of goodness and respectability, but hide their actual hypocrisy and deep intolerance of others?

Or

Are the creatures and people who are different because of their appearance, social status, and the choices they make, the real monsters?

To my nephew, Julian

I will always protect you from those who wear the masks.

"Everything you're looking for lies
behind the mask you wear."
–Stephen C. Paul

Special thanks to Mary J. Nickum,
Sherrie Stoops; Alesha and Gracie.

Contents

You are not who you think you are.
You are not who other people think you are.
You are who you think other people think you are

– EDS

The Maine Gang

Even though I was just a Schnoggin' Knocker, I was still a Monsterjunkie, but I didn't understand what lay ahead—

Close friends, they called themselves the Maine Gang—three boys, Todd, Edgar, and Larry. They enjoyed pushing the envelope in any situation and didn't particularly care who they provoked.

Todd, a sandy-haired, body-builder and actor, was their leader and he posed a provocative question, "Do you guys think we can get into M J Manor and see what's really going on? It's a big property and I think we could like sneak in and check out what's inside. If that bird is just one example, they must have some pretty cool stuff."

Edgar, a short, stocky black youth and aspiring wrestler, added, "My mom and dad think a lot of like strange things are going on there, you know, like animal cloning, weird freaks of nature, that kinda' thing."

Larry, a carrot-top and the school football team quarterback, said, "I know one thing, like that kid's mother is really hot. What's the dork's name? Uh, yeah, Cromwell."

Todd said, "I think he has a sister who's as hot as their mother. We need to make like some plans. I have an idea where we can get in and not be spotted. Are you guys with me?

In unison, Larry and Edgar said, "Let's do it."

∞ 2 ∞

Mysteries and "Monsters"

Nervous, Reggie pulled in front of M J Manor. This enormous Maine estate, an extensive property, was located on the edge of Foggy Point, a quaint seaside community. He was the unfortunate short straw loser for delivery of mail by the United States Postal Service to this address.

As he and several of the other postmen met at the old Post Office, a building built in 1893, they came to a unanimous agreement, they needed one brave person to take sole responsibility for delivering anything and everything to this address—regular mail, special delivery, packages, crates, or whatever. "Just so it's not me," was the prevailing attitude among them.

Finally, four of the most courageous postmen were selected to draw straws, the short straw being the unlucky soul who would make all deliveries to the M J Manor.

Reggie was 'the man,' everyone else applauded him for his courage. At all future get-togethers (the postmen regularly met for drinks and food to play pool at a local pub), he would never be burdened with paying for anything again. Indeed, some genuinely pessimistic types, actually never expected to see him again.

Reggie Orton, an African American with the body of an athlete and an easy sense of humor, usually was non-plussed when it came to delivery. However, delivery to 1313 Road-to-Nowhere was cause for concern. In fact, the entire area and its accompanying monikers, generated some concern and confusion among residents. The avenues, Black Rose Parkway and Sorcerer Avenue were names created by the Conrad Munsterjung family, founders of the great estate, because they were among the first to inhabit this location near Foggy Point in 1913, prior to World War I. The heritage of Conrad Munsterjung was a result of a fortuitous introduction to the 'Mason' organization in Germany at an early adult age. Conrad was fascinated by the group.

Surrounded by verdant indigenous vegetation - wild garlic, leek and ginger, butterfly weed, beach wormwood, salt marsh false-foxglove, Aleutian maidenhair fern. Also, exotic international vegetation surrounded the estate, Australian Wollemi pine (seedlings given as a gift by National Geographic), rat-eating pitcher plant, stinkhorn mushroom, parachute flower, dancing plant, pelican flower, snowdonia hawkweed, waterwheel plant, corpse flower, flypaper plant, dead horse arum lily and *Hydnora Africana*.

Graviola was being grown because of its effectiveness against infections and as an anti-carcinogenic and immune support benefit. Also grown were yellow passion vine, Australian rainbow plant, cobra lily, tropical pitcher plant and other rare plants from around the world. Some were brought back from Vancouver Island, the Philippines, Guatemala, Peru, Columbia, Chili and Brazil, South Africa, Madagascar and Mozambique.

Cycads, a distant relative of the palm, with a stout and woody trunk and a crown of large, hard and stiff, evergreen leaves, grew around the manor. Also, Chinese tallow trees, bamboo and several species of rare palms, brought back by Dr. Monsterjunkie, grew randomly throughout the estate.

An ominous perimeter wall encircled the entire estate, except for the opening to the Atlantic Ocean. Gargoyles staring from the highest points of the six-sided regular-spaced columns made the wall appear ominous. There, a small lagoon, Cryptic Bay, broke inward to a special dock, where mysterious sea creatures visited, some suggested monsters swam into the bay.

A small summer picnic bungalow was located on the shore of Cryptic Bay. As a bungalow, Talon Monsterjunkie's great grandfather, Conrad Monsterjunkie, constructed a facsimile of a British English Tudor vacation home; Isabella Retreat. Conrad honored his beloved wife by naming the bungalow after her, also he was quite fond of the British Isles.

The retreat was constructed in 1914, with imported materials from Estonia, Isabella's childhood home. The pseudo Tudor residence had stone masonry, Estonian limestone and natural boulders, many historic glass windows with Tudor mullions and green moss, growing on slate shingles. Many local birds nested in and around the retreat in the various climbing vines gently caressing the magnificent structure.

Other places on the property included: Black Rose Cottage, a spectacular rose garden and house of the darkest kind; Spider City, a collection of trees completely enveloped in spider webs; Odd Orchard, where extraordinary fruit with brilliantly crafted hybrids grew; Weird Willow, a nesting place for several formidable and strange birds; Varmint Hollow, where the most rare of underground creatures dwelled.

Reggie advanced toward the mailbox, inching his way through a heavy fog to do battle with the mailbox, an entity beyond strange. A creature, the star nosed mole, with big tentacles and beady eyes, often snatched the mail from his shaking hand.

Reggie inhaled deeply, bracing himself for the advance to the mailbox. As he was about to step out of his 1999 Chevy pickup outfitted to deliver mail, he heard a dull thump on top of his vehicle.

"What now?"

Fang, the name given to the mailbox by other delivery people, was chosen because of the two fanged creature with multiple tentacles living inside. The little monster was prone to playfully display his bizarre physiognomy, which frightened most 'normal' people; but, actually, he was quite harmless. It was never identified as a particular living thing, but indeed he was a star nosed mole.

"Good morning Reginald, what is your task?" said the mailbox, telepathically.

Reggie, somewhat surprised and a little disturbed, replied, "Come on, you know I go by Reggie; I haven't been called Reginald, since my great granny aunt insisted when I was a little boy."

"*Oui, oui*, certainly you must know we are a lot more formal in the Monsterjunkie Manor, so do forgive me." The telepathic mole was acquired outside Quebec, Canada, during a speaking tour Dr. Talon Monsterjunkie fulfilled some years back.

Reggie, looking at the very substantial bird dropping on top of his vehicle, asked the mailbox mole, "What kind of flying creature would drop a loaf like that? Man, I got'ta say this pile gives me the creeps, whatever it is… whatever it is, is pretty scary. What is it?"

Once again, telepathically, the mole responded, "*Excusez-moi,* you know that would be telling and I just can not do that."

Reggie, almost pleading, asked, "Can't you just give me a little hint of what **you** are?"

Telepathically, "Now, now, Reggie, you must determine my species yourself, just like everyone communicating with me. If you please, deliver today's mail and, I assure you, the correct family member will receive their correspondence."

Reggie stared at the fangs in the mailbox and could see two recessed eyes staring back at him. He tentatively extended two letters and was startled when a tentacle grabbed them immediately, pulling them in and slamming the opening shut.

He breathed a sigh of relief, until he recalled he must also deliver a crate to the side entrance. He also was disconcerted by the fact that he could hear a dull scratching inside the crate—the contents of which was utterly unknown to him. He just knew that the shipping address was from the South American Amazon country of Brazil.

He inhaled deeply again, this time approaching the gate to the side entrance of the estate. He pressed the call button and held his breath. Soon he heard a reply on the other end, "Ah yes, my delivery from Brazil. I'll open the gate. Pull to the side entrance and please help me un-box it."

Reggie with genuine fear said, "Sir, would you mind telling me what, 'it,' is?"

"It's Lacuna, our new pet; we'll be the first lucky ones to see him revived from the shipping crate. He is a splendid creature, a Goliath bird eater and I'm sure you'll love him as much as I do. See you promptly."

When the gate opened, Reggie eased his vehicle forward and proceeded down the fog-shrouded road to the entrance. What became progressively more disturbing to him was the scratching sound within the crate, which was getting louder and louder, as if what was inside, knew it was about to be liberated. He finally arrived at the delivery portal of the great house where he saw, standing in the fog, the tall figure of Talon Monsterjunkie. He eased his truck around to where he and Talon could pull off the crate safely. He experienced an odd mixture of dread and curiosity about the crate's contents.

Talon stood smiling in the fog observing Reggie's entrance to the loading dock. His latest acquisition, an extraordinary creature he captured in the Amazon jungle, one of the many places an active cryptozoologist would find the rarest and, in many cases, mythical, thought-to-be-non-existent, creatures of the planet. His driving ambition was the 'living world,' which led him from one adventure to another. However, his deepest passion was cryptozoology, or the location and capture of the impossibly odd denizens of the world—animals most people do not believe actually exist.

He, a tall slender raven-haired specimen, was athletic, handsome and extremely intelligent. He was the most popular lecturer in the Maine College Biology Department, where he was idolized by his students, but viewed suspiciously by some of his colleagues. Dr. Monsterjunkie often travelled beyond rigid academic boundaries into mysteries, with which many were uncomfortable dealing.

He and Reggie unloaded the crate and Reggie stood back as he pried open the top. Talon spoke to his new arrival, "Welcome to M J Manor, my friend." As he fished some grain from his lab coat, he

8

placed the seeds in his open palm into the box, where a gentle munching sound was now the only sound heard.

Reggie backed off a little more as he saw two hairy arms extend over the top of the box. Somewhat concerned, he backed off even further. His eyes bulged wide at what he saw next. As Talon stepped back and continued to hold his hand out, the box's cargo now became apparent, when out crawled a spider with eight enormous hairy legs—a gigantic specimen of its kind. The spider had eight enormous legs supporting a rather petite body with a smaller head and multiple eyes, primarily black.

Reggie babbled, "What . . . What. . . What in the world is that?"

Seeing his fear, Talon reassured him, "Trust me, this is a friendly, lovely creature, who would never harm anyone. Look at him, isn't he beautiful? What exquisite symmetry, look at the perfectly proportioned legs—absolute poetry in motion. Would you care to pet him, Reggie?"

Reggie horrified, shouted, "Oh, Lordy, Lordy, Lordy. If I hadn't seen it, I wouldn't have believed it. Sorry Dr. Monsterjunkie, I have to finish my route. I've gotta go now, thank you." Reggie left and didn't look back.

Unperturbed, Talon led Lacuna into the main hall of the estate, where Pandora greeted him and his latest acquisition. Pandora, his wife, was raven-haired with an alabaster complexion, which made her full red lips seem even brighter. Enveloped in the sensuous scents of jasmine and lavender, she was stunning and perfectly proportioned. When she entered a room, both men and women were stopped in their tracks.

She said, "What an astonishing creature. Is there anything like him anywhere in the world?"

Talon replied, "I don't think so. He is without question the largest example of his species I've ever observed."

Pandora praised him, saying, "Without a doubt, you're the most talented cryptozoologist on the planet. I think you attract creatures like this just like a magnet and they're all unique. And some people think of them as monsters, most incredible."

Talon, smiling, said, "I attracted you, my greatest find, dear."

"You're too kind Tal, but I still appreciate the compliment." Pulling the letter from the school envelope and handing it to Talon, she said, "I've just read the letter we got from Cromwell's school today. He has some problems we need to discuss."

"Oh yes, I see," he said as he studied the letter. "Do you suppose he is shy and reserved because of bullying?" asked Talon.

"It could be," replied Pandora. "I do know one thing, I need to get more involved with his school. I'm going to attend a 'What-do-your-parents-do?' session in his class, and I also plan to attend a PTA meeting in the near future."

"That should be interesting, Pan. Be careful not to give away too much about our special hobbies, OK?"

Pandora replied, "Perhaps that's part of the problem. I know we value our privacy, but how that is affecting Cromwell is another matter."

∞ 3 ∞

What's in a Name?

Cromwell, or Crow as he preferred, roamed the grounds of M J Manor, considering his life. He'd inherited a sensitive, intelligent face along with a shock of black hair from his mother and father. Crow always dressed in black clothing, down to his black sueded lace-up Creeper shoes. His black hair was spiked and he wore a set of silver earrings.

He despised his name and asked to be called Crow, which his parents never seemed to understand, because Talon and Pandora always preferred formality. To understand, Crow had a traumatic childhood. His Cromwellian designation by classmates was used mercilessly to tease and harass him.

The association with the Monsterjunkie name was enough to cause his peers to look down on him. The logo, 'M J', depicted above the entry gate, also provided fuel for the constant teasing of the school pranksters. His classmates did monstrous imitations of the image. His most cherished pet, a rare, white raven named Malikai, had just come to rest on his shoulder. This white raven was his companion on the estate, which he often admitted into his bedroom. Crow wanted to believe the white raven was a messenger from the Great Spirit, of which he'd read in Native American mythology.

He was an unhappy boy who felt isolated, because he was unable to make friends at school. He spent a lot of time playing with and being consoled by the "monsters." In fact, the so-called monsters were his only real friends.

The names at school directed at him were starting to become more frequent and more cutting. "Goth" and "creep" were now added to the descriptors that he could hear whispered about him, along with the comments on the general weirdness of M J Manor.

Along with this, was the awakening of his body to early adolescence and the first confusing undefined feelings of his sexuality.

His walk took him to a most unusual doghouse, Chico, a genuine chupacabra, was the near mythical, but nevertheless real creature that roamed the Mexican highlands. He was ferocious looking, but his actual behavior was more like a dog. Chico jumped from his house with a rubber ball in his mouth and advanced to Crow with his strange whining muffled bark, which always indicated he wanted to play.

Crow smiled at him, took the ball from his mouth and tossed it deep into the woods, as Chico dashed after it. Chico returned shortly with it and Crow tossed it one more time before he moved on.

He spotted Frances and Betty, identical twins, pituitary giants, who were the jacks-of-all-trade caretakers of the manor. They put down their pails of 'monster' food, greeted him warmly and knelt down to give him a gentle embrace.

"How are we doing today, Crow?" asked Betty.

"I'm alright, I guess."

"You seem a little down. Can we help?" asked Frances.

"Same old, same old, school sucks, just like my life. I'm either bored, lonely or pissed off, because I only have the folks around here to talk to. I guess I shouldn't complain; it's better than nothing."

Betty said, "You deserve a lot more. We know what a great kid you are and things can always change."

"Thanks, I sure hope so. See you all later," as the two giants walked another path to continue their feeding of the creatures in this unique sanctuary.

Crow heard the continuous thud of a tennis ball hitting a backboard and thought, '*That must be Beauregard practicing, he's somebody I could talk to.*' He continued his walk and spotted Beauregard, a sasquatch, his father had raised from infancy, leaving the only tennis court on the property.

He ambled over to him and wished him a good morning. Beauregard was discovered by Talon in the Canadian wilderness when he was only a few months old. He had found him alone on an isolated lakeshore with no parent anywhere around. He was undernourished, apparently there had been no parent around him for some time. Talon loaded him onto his hydroplane and flew him back to Maine, where he was raised on the estate.

As Crow grew, he and Beauregard had become close friends. Beau was content living in isolation on the M J Manor property. His true love was reading, writing poetry, and an occasional tennis match with one of the others.

Crow exclaimed, "Where did you come by your tennis sweater? That's a cool design. It matches your fur."

"Thanks for that, young Crow Master. I see your companion sits well on your shoulder." Malikai acknowledged his compliment with an approving squawk. "I've got something to show you. Join me at my cottage."

They walked a short distance to Beauregard's cottage, where the two seated themselves in his small living room. "I've written a poem in your honor," Beau announced. "Allow me to read it to you, before I hand you the scroll that's yours to keep."

"Wow, Beau, thanks. Go ahead."

Beau rolled out the scroll and began:

Young Cromwell, one best known as Crow,
a darkness follows you wherever you go.
Fear not the inky feelings you have inside,
the shadows there will not rule, or survive.

The white raven is your truth to its core,
an untold love of nature, like his, you adore.
Like the joyful flight of your white friend
your frayed self can soar to greater ends.

This time of darkness is but a tiny phase,
your true self will rise like light above haze.
Choose coming allies and friends with care,
with them, fix on hope, then seek and dare.

Crow beamed with joy and a tear glistened in his eye with this recitation and exclaimed, "That was awesome. I'll put this in my secret box. I can't thank you enough, Beau."

"Just seeing you smile is thanks enough, young man. Take those words to heart, especially the last two lines. I believe things are about to change for you."

Crow exclaimed, "Thanks again. This, this makes my day," as he resumed his stroll across the grounds. In the distance he could see a stirring in a great tree, Weird Willow, right in the center of the property. He thought, *I wonder what's up with Periwinkle.* He walked to the base of the tree and looked skyward, as some large droppings just missed him.

He shouted, "Periwinkle, come down now."

Periwinkle, one of his dad's great discoveries, culminated in a search he conducted on an isolated Indonesian island, Good Enough Island, where rumors of Pterodactyls had existed for decades. He found a very young Pterodactyl in one of the highland areas, struggling with an injured leg. When he finally returned to Maine, Pandora garlanded the young bird's first nest with exquisite flowers, the purples and blues of periwinkles, hence her unique name.

The enormous bird sprang from her nest, took a single glide around Weird Willow and landed in front of Crow. With a sheepish look on her face—as sheepish as a Pterodactyl could look—she stretched her head toward him so he could stroke her.

He did so while asking, "What's wrong, Peri? Do you have a serious digestive problem? We've gotten more than a few complaints, including Reggie, the postal guy." Pointing to a couple of vultures sitting in the tree branches, he asked, "Ugh, You didn't change your diet did you?" She shook her head no, and with a look of pride, she looked down at her nest.

Crow said, "Oh my goodness, did you lay an egg? What kind of a bird could knock up a Pterodactyl?"

She sheepishly pointed to the top of the tree, where an enormous Dodo bird sat triumphantly, staring down at his true love. A stupefied Crow said, "You did it with a Dodo? They didn't name this tree Weird Willow for nothing. How could you? How will something like that look? Oh, my God, I'm starting to sound like my parents. Wow. Wait 'till I tell them this. Since you and the Dodo are living together, have you started to plan for the little whatever?" Peri smiling, nodded yes, with great pride.

"OK, Peri, but be a little more careful where you make your deposits, OK?"

She smiled, as Crow hugged her, "It's alright girl, I guess you can't hold back love, a concept I'm not even close to figuring out myself, so I guess I'll shut up on the subject. See ya' soon." He continued his trek, shaking his head in disbelief at what he'd just seen.

✄ 4 ✄

Parent Occupations

Prior to Pandora's arrival at the special class, 'Parent Occupations', Crow sat alone anxiously awaiting the arrival of his mother, who was always late, fashionably or otherwise. Two parents had already explained their occupations. He felt the sting of some whispered barbs about what "weirdo's" parents must look like. He regretted that his father, Talon, could not attend, because he had a class at Maine College, which conflicted.

Pandora entered the class as the next parent was about to speak. More eyes were focused on her than the mother who went to the podium to explain her nursing profession. To say Pandora was gorgeous was an understatement. She could do more things with black than most people could do with an entire array of colors. Her full-length dress, a Debbie Pencil skirt with a matching black blouse and a perfectly selected strikingly patterned scarf announced her presence. Her simply designed outfit clung to her well-proportioned body, like skin on a peach. Her overcoat and its collar, which artfully framed her raven hair and alabaster face, subtly exhibited the shape beneath—it was nearly impossible to avert one's eyes from her.

She sat down by Crow, observing the setting. People glanced away from her as she tried to engage eye contact with them. She said nothing to Crow and waited patiently for her turn to speak. When her time to speak arrived, she stood up, removed her overcoat and asked Crow to open a window.

She went to the podium to speak, "Thank you for inviting me to speak today, Mr. Hodges." As she observed Crow open the window, "My name is Pandora Monsterjunkie, and I work with my husband in a field that has very few specialists—cryptozoology. For those of you who have never heard the term, it simply means we find animals that are thought to be extinct, or supposedly live in mythical lore. We work to sustain them and, if possible, assist their breeding."

"Better than just talking about these creatures, I've brought one with me today that was thought to be extinct. My husband, Dr. Talon Monsterjunkie, found him on an isolated fjord on the South Island of New Zealand. Dr. Monsterjunkie has an uncanny ability to attract these wonderful, but very rare creatures. It's as if he gives off a vibration that animals understand and feel safe—not just any animals, but more often, isolated creatures, who would otherwise be extremely wary of any human contact.

"I bring you such a creature today." She walked over to her overcoat and withdrew a large falconer's glove and started a music recording of an accordion playing an old New Zealand melody. Pandora began making a series of loud whistle shrieks standing by the window. Then she projected a very melancholy hooting sound through the same window.

Suddenly, as if out of nowhere, a laughing owl alighted on the windowsill, to the gasps of the audience. Pandora advanced to the magnificent 'free' creature, whose combination of yellow, brown, white and maroon stripes ran the length of his body and wings. Pandora greeted him, "Welcome to this gathering, 'Chuckles,'" as she stroked his large breast. Addressing the audience she said, "Soon you'll see why he has this name."

Suddenly Chuckles began a strangely muted laugh that turned into a gentle, low mewing. Then he made a sound that could only be characterized as a small dog barking. It surprised and delighted everyone in the room.

A question came up from a student in the back who asked, "Why did you play the accordion music before he came to the window?"

"At the turn of the last century, people in New Zealand attracted them to their homes, using accordion music. No one knew for sure why that happened, but some animals seem to respond to certain sounds." She continued, "He is very inquisitive about this place and, if you allow him, he'll peacefully walk the table here and check out the audience. Don't be concerned, Chuckles won't bite."

She placed him down on the table in front of the podium and the owl began walking its length. "Will he talk to us?" came a question.

"Not talking by our standards but you may pick up an inference or two by how he answers you." Looking at a girl he was approaching, Pandora said to her, "Give it a try."

Chuckles stopped in front of her and, smiling, she asked, "Chuckles, do you like my dress?"

Chuckles cocked his head towards her, as if he was trying to speak and then he began the deep strange laugh he'd first exhibited. Everyone in the room joined him in laughter.

The girl said, "I guess I should like take that as a 'yes.'"

Pandora began to take questions from more people in the audience and she finally heard the one she anticipated. "Why don't you make M J Manor more... more available to Foggy Point, more available to the world?" She had already rehearsed a response that she and Talon had delivered many times to people who had an overripe desire to explore the mysteries of their grounds. She said, "M J Manor is a very special kind of sanctuary with extraordinary creatures. Many of them are very solitary and would be threatened by even well intentioned people. Dr. Monsterjunkie is a licensed veterinarian and caring for them and teaching throughout the world consume much of his time, as it does mine. We have occasional visitors and, perhaps someday, if conditions were right, we'd entertain more, but that's not in our immediate plans."

Chuckles moved to a boy at the end of the table. He somewhat reluctantly asked, "If this guy is like many of the animals you have, any chance of pulling some part time work to help you all out? Also, are there any animals at your place that are really scary or dangerous?"

Pandora smiled at him and said, "Thanks for the offer but we're OK for help, and as far as your second question goes, we've never had anyone injured by an animal we shelter. Are they scary? It depends on your point of view—certainly none of them are to us."

Pandora moved Chuckles to the next long table, where he began his walk again. Pausing in front of the nurse who had talked earlier, she asked, "May I pet him the way you did earlier?" Pandora answered, "Of course." The nurse stroked him the full length of his multi colored breast and Chuckles presented the audience with a new sound, a childlike cooing, which warmly bonded everybody to this special owl.

The last person at the end of the table was Crow. Chuckles immediately acknowledged him by jumping on his shoulder, where he occasionally rode, when Crow's regular shoulder companion was elsewhere. Crow didn't want to be the center of attention, but, at this point, he was the unavoidable focus of all of his classmates. He scrutinized their glances and, in many of their faces, he saw something besides indifference or contempt. He really wasn't sure what he saw. He knew his mother would make a strong impression—she always did, especially among males. He also did know one thing— that much to his discomfort, people would want to know more about him—him and the truth about M J Manor and its alleged "monsters."

After the presentations, Ed Hodges, one of the parents who attended, approached Pandora and introduced himself. Ed looked out-of-place in Levis with his name inscribed in lapidary on his belt with a silver belt buckle, a work shirt with a t-shirt and cowboy boots. A bit intimidated by her beauty, he said, "It's a pleasure to meet you, Mrs. Monsterjunkie. Would you consider attending one of our PTA meetings?"

Pandora said, "Excellent idea, actually, I was already planning to attend, but thanks for the invitation anyway. You'll have to excuse me, I must be going." She walked over to Crow, with a small gathering of classmates around him, and retrieved Chuckles. She said to Crow, "Please walk with me to the car."

Crow, rather surprised said, "Of course."

As she opened the hatchback and placed Chuckles on the perch in his cage, she asked, "How do you think your classmates reacted to this?"

"As usual, you were a hit, Mother."

"I noticed several students gathered around you after the talk. What were they saying?"

"They were impressed. I hope you realize this will bring more attention to us.

How do you feel about that?"

Pandora thoughtfully paused and said, "Maybe it's time we become somewhat better known. I'm going to the PTA meeting and that will give me a chance to feel things out. Give me a kiss good bye. I'll see you later."

Unobserved from the same window that Chuckles landed in the classroom, three of Crow's classmates observed this scene and talked among themselves.

∞ 5 ∞

The Color of Excellence

Indigo, Talon and Pandora's daughter, was named by her father because of her rare, deep-blue eyes, and by Pandora because of her precocity and passionate curiosity, which was evident from birth. She chose to dye her black hair purple and usually dressed in black with fishnet stockings and high-topped black platform boots.

Now in high school, where she was an outstanding student, Indigo had adapted to the "strangeness" of M J Manor, based on her strong intuition about people and her ability to communicate. She was socially comfortable, despite her obvious gifts and, although she had several friends, she had no true confidants.

Her teachers and peers, after getting to know her, simply dismissed her connection to M J Manor. When she invited an occasional visitor to the manor, it was always within restricted parameters, ones that did not disclose the creatures contained within its walls.

The evening that Pandora was to go to the PTA meeting, Indigo approached her with a request. Staring at her with her hypnotically deep blue eyes, she said, "I want to go with you to the meeting tonight."

Pandora, surprised by the request, said, "Of course, but I'm curious why you want to go? This doesn't look like you're cup of tea." Then, suddenly, Pandora realized something she had become used to with Indigo, her acute sense of how things could unfold, some would call a prophetic gift. She smiled at her and said, "Something tells me this is going to be an interesting meeting."

"Can you give me a hint, Indy?"

"Oh, it's just a feeling, Mother. You know how I am."

Pandora laughed, "Well, I guess we'll just leave it at that."

That evening, Pandora and Indigo arrived at the PTA meeting, only slightly late, mostly because Indigo insisted they get to the meeting on time. Ed Hodges, dressed comfortably as usual, was at the podium talking to the group; the same Ed Hodges who had invited Pandora to this meeting, was discussing his role in controlling school bullying. He had joined a committee recently, after he, his daughter, Winter, and his son, Mark arrived in the community. His face lit up when he saw Pandora enter the room.

A widower, who had lost his wife in a car accident, Ed decided to pull up stakes and start afresh in New England. His daughter, Winter, was just getting her bearings in school, in an environment far less threatening than the school she had attended before. She'd been a victim of bullying, mostly because of her unconventional dress, too "Goth" for the cliquish types that belonged to her former school.

Winter was a good student, cultivating a genuine talent in art and loved sketching anywhere, anytime. She sat in the audience meticulously penciling in her father at the PTA podium in her electronic sketchbook, ISketch.

Ed's conservative talk concluded and he returned to his seat by his daughter. Winter understood, since her mother died, her father was experiencing difficulty relating to others, after all he'd lost the love of his life. Winter graciously shared her sketch and he smiled,

"Good job honey, my cheeks are a little bit full, aren't they? Have I gained that much weight?"

"Yep, too much clam chowder, Dad. You're gon'na have to cut down."

Ed asked in a reserved manner, "What did you think of my talk on bullying?"

"You hit it. If you ever need any testimonials, I'll be glad to provide them."

Ed said, "Look over your shoulder at the woman sitting in the back row. She was the one who brought the laughing owl to Mark's class, an impressive creature.

Actually, it was all Mark could talk about when we got home. I wonder if that's her daughter sitting by her. We need to introduce ourselves at the end of the meeting."

"Whatever, Dad."

They waited for the conclusion of the meeting. Pandora was talking to several people, some of whom had attended her presentation. Indigo had noticed Winter sketching. Breaking away from Pandora's group, Indigo approached her and introduced herself.

"Hi, I'm Indigo, are you sketching. Do you mind if I have a look?"

Winter smiled as she handed her ISketch to Indigo, "Sure, check out my father, does that look like him?"

Indigo, impressed, exclaimed, "Wow, that's like very realistic. Art's your gig, you're sick."

"My name is Winter and this is my dad, Ed Hodges. Was the woman sitting by you, your mother? My brother Mark talked nonstop about the bird she brought to class. What a sick animal."

Indigo said, "My brother is like in the same class. His name's Cromwell, but he calls himself Crow." Turning to Ed, she said, "I wonder if my mom and I could talk to you about bullying sometime. We think Crow may be the target of some of it."

"Anytime, and I guess that could concern Mark too, since he is in the same class as your brother. We are relatively new to the area and don't know many people, so I think it's a good idea."

Indigo asked Winter, "Do you have your school lunch break around noon? You want to get together and talk?"

"Noon it is. That's my lunch hour, too."

Watching Pandora conclude her talk with the other parents, she gestured to Indigo she was ready to leave. "I just saw my mom give me a signal, she wants to leave. Thanks for your speech, Mr. Hodges. It's given me a lot to think about. See ya' tomorrow, Winter."

∝∽ 6 ∝∽

Conrad's Determination

Conrad stood on the porch of his massive Bavarian lodge, staring at the sun setting in the west. He was moved, as his emotions fluttered back and forth between nostalgic sadness and exuberant excitement—all of this focused on a powerful decision he had made. He knew he must leave this beautiful land, his home and the home of countless generations of Munsterjungs who walked the lush mountain valleys and forests of this land. Preparations were complete and now the time had come.

A passionate apprentice of the created world, especially the inexplicable oddities of the hidden mysteries of this planet, he was also a wary and astute student of human existence. A terrible dread was growing about the tendencies of European governments to obsessively elevate their influence on their neighboring countries. At this time in the early years of the 20th century, this sickness, which would later be called nationalism, or its twin brother, imperialism, was beginning to envelope his land—and, at a visceral level of understanding, he knew it would ultimately destroy much of what he cherished.

It had already killed his oldest brother in one of the many pointless wars that were springing up like black roses of death on the land of Europa. His beloved Reinhold, who having been one of his closest friends and mentors perished in the Franco Prussian War, a chest beating exercise in the "balance of power" and checker board land swapping in the 1870's. It grieved and sickened Conrad and planted the seeds of dissent to move away from this "new world order."

He became deeply enamored with the United States of America, previously engaging in two major trips to America. He took his wife, Isabella, on the second journey. She, too, fell in love with this relatively new country, especially the coastal area of New England. Nevertheless, contemplating the complete displacement of family, shattering ancient family history by abandoning Europe, was a painful path. However, Conrad's sense of adventure won the battle of contradictory emotions.

Standing on his Bavarian balcony, enjoying the flowers blooming in the planting boxes along the banister, he realized this could well be the last time he would witness the joy of this land. Tears began to well up and, shortly, Isabella joined him to share the pleasant view. She felt his pathos deeply as she embraced him and said tenderly, "Be at peace with yourself, dear husband, if your father, Wolfgang, had faced comparable circumstances, he would do as your are doing. Indeed, it is better neither of your parents lived to witness your brother's death.

"We have experienced the land we're going to and it is a better place than the world we are leaving. Even the president there loves life and loves the land. He took a vast area of their west and made it into a protected park. He has such a charming name—Teddy, it's so wonderful they've named toy bears after him. Find such a leader in Europe who would have such a name. Of course, you wouldn't. Some of them would be better named for the monsters of brutal nightmares that they are."

They held each other as their warmth and love mingled with their tears in the fading daylight that transitioned into night in this 'old world.' Soon they would be absorbed in building a manor house on an estate in the new world.

⧂ 7 ⧂

Monsters — Really?

D r. Talon Monsterjunkie was an award winning teacher and researcher. He was passionate about his work, which in the big picture of his life, was the description and presentation of the living world to students. But, in a more specific sense, it was the exercise of a special talent—attracting and collecting some of nature's most unusual oddities. His methods and unexpected surprises in the classroom matched his spontaneous personality and his willingness to cleverly improvise, depending on the animal about which he was teaching. One of the most popular teachers at Maine College, his classrooms, typically, were always over booked, much to the chagrin of some the older and more traditional faculty members.

Professor Monsterjunkie stood in front of his class in his typical dark clothing, glasses perched on his nose, ready to field a question from one of his students. The student asked, "Sir, where does your name derive from? It looks like just a combination of Monster and Junkie - addicted to monsters."

Talon smiled and responded, "That is probably very close to my mind set, except the monster part has no negative connotation, because I love the so-called 'monsters.' It's literally from the German. When my great grandfather, Conrad Munsterjung, left Germany to live in the United States, he wanted a name that was more Americanized. Translated from the German, "Munsterjung," means young cheese, not the most glamorous, or pleasantly odorous moniker to wear." Several students laughed at the inference.

He continued, "Conrad was the first in our family to pursue cryptozoology and, consequentially, the name translated very nicely, in his mind at least, to Monsterjunkie. Indeed, one addicted to monsters, a name that had a very positive connection for him and still does for our family."

He continued, "So, what is a monster? I'm sure, when that African fisherman captured a Coelacanth in his net, the first question was probably, 'Is this a prehistoric monster? What kind of monster is this?' Of course, it wasn't a monster, just a creature thought to be extinct, but was very much alive.

"The gorilla and the giant squid were both thought to be myths, but in fact are quite real. Even another human species, such as the Hobbits of Southeast Asia, existed and other primate or primate-type creatures have been spotted on obscure islands.

"New species of things are constantly being discovered. Now, there is a Top Ten New Animals Discovered list that's published every year. The point here is, the living world is filled with surprises—surprises, which can delight us, puzzle us or, in some cases, scare the hell out of us. Life is phenomenally creative; it dishes up extraordinary diversity and is wonderfully unpredictable.

"Today, I have something here that will stretch your imagination, when I describe it verbally, and then when you actually see it. Be honest about your reactions. Oh, by the way, don't use your smart phones to research, until we've talked this through. Can you name me some of the giant monsters from those old 50's horror classics—anybody?"

Hands began shooting up, "The Fly." "The Blob." "The one with the giant ants, I can't remember the name." "The Creature from the Black Lagoon." "The Thing." "Godzilla."

OK, good, but does anyone remember a giant arachnid?

Another hand went up and answered the question, "Earth Versus the Spider."

Dr. Monsterjunkie added to this response saying, "'Tarantula' and 'The Giant Spider Invasion' were two more. This was the 'atomic age' and suddenly radiated bugs grew to giant proportions and turned into monsters. Spiders, to many people, are terrible creatures and giant ones touch some primal fear inside us. Maybe the best modern representation of that was 'Shelob,' in the *Return of the King*. I know some people who had trouble watching it. Be honest, "How many of you are afraid of spiders? And I realize many of you are biology majors."

About a third of the class raised their hands. He said, "That's nothing to be ashamed of, sometimes in the field, especially in a remote place, I must deal with fear of some of the creatures I encounter."

After a long pause, while he brought a crate to the front of the class, he finally spoke, "Today I'm going to release a giant spider into this class." He let the remark sink in, as he judged the affect on students in the class. He detected no obvious fear, but certainly some nervousness on the part of a number of class members.

"This is the largest known Goliath bird eater, a specimen with a diameter of over two feet. I now think of him as a pet. In fact he has a name—Lacuna." Talon opened the crate and, after a short wait, Lacuna emerged from the top and dropped on to the floor. The students were riveted to its movements. As Dr. Monsterjunkie approached, it raised its front legs, while he grabbed a handful of a special feed from a paper bag.

Professor Monsterjunkie asked, "Would anyone like to feed him?"

The student, who asked him about his name origin, volunteered, "Let me, sir."

He advanced to the spider carefully, as Dr. Monsterjunkie gave him a handful of a special meal he had concocted for the spider's diet. Dr. Monsterjunkie said, "Go ahead, he'll take the food right from your hand."

Everybody watched carefully, as the spider slowly consumed his special meal from the student's palm. When the spider finished, the student returned to his seat beaming with happiness for accomplishing what few people had ever attempted.

Next, Professor Monsterjunkie asked, "Would anyone like to pet Lacuna." A girl in the front row immediately volunteered. She went forward and carefully stroked the spider's head and commented, "His hair is amazingly soft." Not long after commenting, she returned to her seat.

Dr. Monsterjunkie asked the class, "Can anyone tell me how many people have died from a Goliath bite?"

A student in the back of the class answered, "Professor, I'm just guessing, but I'd say the answer is zero."

"You guessed correctly, young man. The death toll from any Goliath or tarantula bite is exactly zero. I can't give you an accurate count on the casualties from radiation-induced giant spiders, but I suspect it's the same amount."

As he placed Lacuna back in the crate, he declared, "Part of this demonstration is about perception and the culture that produces 'monsters' completely from our imaginative fears and nightmares. Look at the animals that have been demonized by popular culture: bats, wolves, mountain lions, and sharks, to just name a few. The point of this is, there are no monsters just animals that perform some of their natural functions in ways that aren't compatible with our myths or customs. Always remember, when you systematically remove animals from an ecosystem, you unbalance the very system you are trying to protect."

"Well, enough of cryptozoology and special animals, let's move on to the issue of protecting ecosystems, which is the subject of today's discussion."

8

The Persistence of Labels

Winter and Indigo found a comfortable private place for lunch, where they could talk. Indigo asked her, "How are things going for you here? I know you've been in town for only a few months and I've seen how weird it is getting used to a new school."

"This place is so much better than where I was. You have no idea. It was clique city where you were either a jock, a cheerleader, a nerd, a preppie, a punk, gay, a dyke, a hippie, Goth, a cowboy, a gangsta, or a slut—do you get the picture? It was a big school, literally thousands and most people felt they had to 'belong' to something."

She exhaled and continued, "I felt completely out of place. Where does an art student go, when she doesn't care about playing out some stupid role that doesn't fit into one of those slots. I got the label of either 'Goth' or 'dyke' put on me just by the way I dressed— mostly by people who were clueless about who I really was and wouldn't know good clothing from the fifties fab. When the bullying started, my dad decided it was time to move on.

"You might have noticed, my dad is fairly reserved. I was so glad he got a job in this town. This area is so different from where I was. What about you? I've heard some pretty strange stuff about your estate. My dad manages the UPS branch for this area, the same thing he did before. He said they had to draw straws to see who would deliver to your place."

Indigo laughed and said, "That doesn't surprise me at all. A cryptozoologist brings in some crazy stuff and the place we live is a kind of improvised zoo—then there's the mailbox—and I don't know how to describe what that is. I can see why delivery people get nervous around our place. I guess I'm kinda' lucky, Maine is filled with a lot of like independent types. My grandfather came here many years ago and people got used to our so-called 'strangeness.' I've noticed some of the things you talked about, but we're a much smaller school and the only thing that's cropped up this year is the threat of bullying, we're not really sure how bad it is."

"The place you live must be really cool. My brother, Mark, was so excited about that bird—the laughing owl, he called it—he wouldn't shut up about it. Your parents lead such interesting lives. It must be great fun."

"Yea, a mixed bag. My father is away a lot, but I'm pretty close to my mother and I get along with my kid brother, Crow—his preferred name, by the way. He can't stand Cromwell and I've decide to push my mom and dad to call him what he wants to be called. Know what I mean?"

"Completely, but I've never had any nicknames, I actually like Winter."

"It's a cool name. I think it's neat to name your kids after like one of the seasons, maybe the one you were born in." Indigo asked, "Were you like born in a winter month?"

"Actually I was, but strangely enough, I never made that connection. You're named after a color. What an awesome thing to do. So, you were talking about bullying, as something new to you. I assume it's directed at Crow and you'd like to do something about it. The only thing I have to go on is my experience.

"When people got into the nasty name-calling and personal threats—you know, the real haters and the goobers that hang with them—I went to my dad immediately. Hey, I wasn't about to like get into the go-it-alone, tough-it-out crap, so I went to my teachers, and gave them a heads up, along with an assistant principal. He helped things, but it didn't help me change my foreign connection with the school, I thought I was from Paris or something.

"If the jam is bad, first thing you need to do is what my dad did. This is a much smaller school and you've been in this community for a long time, with you father's clout, I bet you'd snip it yesterday. "

"That's good, but I also want to be in the groove, when our brothers can't, we need to speak real, bullying is bad mojo. Winter, you can help me figure out what to do, is that the way?"

"Sure, no prob."

Indigo asked, "What's your mom like?"

"She's dead. She was killed by a drunk driver a little over two years ago, we never found anything out."

"Oh my goodness, sorry."

"It's OK. You wouldn't have known. I miss her, she understood me, my mother's name was Keitha."

A short period of time passed to allow Winter's heart to sigh.

"What do you think of the school here?"

"It's an epic improvement over where I was. I really relate to the art teacher; she is a way-cool free spirit, but really knows her stuff.

I've learned a lot from her already. Foggy Point is a cool place, very few a—holes."

Indigo smiled and said, "Let's get together at my place sometime. My parents are very private, but I think I can pull it off. Trust me, my house is never boring. Let's get set up on Twitter and email, so we can talk. Lunch is over."

Winter, intrigued by the possibility of visiting M J Manor said, "Cool, I'll do the same on my phone."

∝ 9 ∝

Intruders

Todd, Larry, and Edgar each successfully snuck out of their respective homes and met at their agreed-upon starting point, a massive oak tree, not far from M J Manor, on the Road to No Where. Each was dressed in black, wearing a black ski hat.

The three huddled around the base of the ancient oak. Todd, whispering, said, "OK, you guys good to go?" Edgar and Larry nodded yes, as Todd continued to speak, "We're going to work around the estate wall until we get like close to the ocean. There's a big overhanging tree there that we can easily climb. It'll be a piece of cake to get inside. I like scouted the area a couple of months ago."

Edgar, a little nervous said, "What do you think is in there?"

Larry said, "I've heard rumors of some giant bird that lives in one of the old trees. I've also heard there's a big ape that like roams the property."

Todd, a little peeved with them, said, "You sound afraid; you're not gon'na turn chicken on me now, are you?"

Larry and Edgar simultaneously snorted, "No way."

They carefully moved to the spooky wall surrounding the estate. Todd pointed at the gargoyles staring down from the top of the multi-sided columns along the wall.

"Wonder whose idea that was?"

They began working their way along the wall. The wall was covered with various vines and mosses. After a couple hundred yards, they halted suddenly when they heard a strange noise from a branch that extended over the wall of the estate. Just above them, a great grey owl hooted mournfully at their approach as he studied the three carefully. The great grey was quite different from the laughing owl, much less colorful, primarily multi-colored grey and various shades of brown. His fixed eyes made the three uncomfortable as they hurried their pace. A short time later, they heard the waves of the Atlantic lap up against the shore in the distance. The three spotted the tree they would climb to get to the other side of the wall.

When they got to the trunk, Todd said, "Follow me, I have a pretty good idea how this will work." An easily climbable tree, the three reached a vantage point where they could look over the wall with a clear view. Down the oceanfront, they could just discern an old world house on a small cove not far from the beach.

Todd said, "Wow, I didn't know this place existed. Let's check it out." They jumped from a branch that reached over the wall and hung down almost to the ground inside the estate. With a fairly sharp drop off, the branch became U-shaped on the other side and allowed them to jump comfortably onto the grounds.

Todd said, "Come on, let's check this place out." Stealthily, they moved along the beach, well away from the shoreline. The three halted immediately as they heard a thrashing sound in the water about 20 or 30 yards out. On extreme alert, the three quickly moved behind a large driftwood trunk and peaked over the top, trying to see what made the sound.

Their eyes widened in awe as they witnessed an enormous sea serpent raise its head high above the water. Its wide mouth fixed in what looked like a bizarre smile, it looked landward and then flopped into the ocean, leaving a wake behind it as it headed for the cove with the house.

Larry excitedly exclaimed, "That… was that a sea monster."

Edgar kept on repeating, "Wow, Wow, Wow."

"We haven't been inland and already we've seen a real sea monster," as Todd grabbed the two and jumped for joy. "Let's go, if this is what we can expect, tonight will be awesome."

As the three got closer to the beach house, they grew cautious when they saw a dim light on the dock in front of the house. While they inched their way forward, they could just barely discern something in the water being joined by what looked like some kind of inflatable thing.

When they arrived on the other side of the dock in the cove just across from the two things they observed before, they still could not see a clear image. Before they could ask each other a question, the water exploded in front of them. Standing before them was the sea monster they'd seen earlier. No more than 15 feet away in the water, it slowly advanced in their direction.

Todd shouted, "Run, run for your lives." They fled toward the interior, as the sea monster with a curious smile on its face, puzzling at their behavior, withdrew back into the water.

Crow was on the other side of the compound, studying the stars from a little tree house the twins had built for him when he heard Todd's shout. They had never had any intruders before and he ran in the direction of the shout to investigate, knowing it was somewhere near Bizarre Beach. From a vantage point of high ground not far from the tree house, he could see three figures in the distance walking to an area his family called Odd Orchard. It was Talon's collection of hybridized trees and oddities that would puzzle even the most experienced arborists. He decided to enlist Beauregard to investigate who these people were.

The three had no idea where they were going. Todd finally stopped them and said, "Slow down. Hold up. That thing scared the crap out of me too, but it's not following us on land."

Edgar said, "This looks like an orchard."

Larry asked, as he studied an odd tree, "What kind of fruit is this? They all look different"

"I have no idea," replied Todd.

A full moon now illuminated the entire orchard and they came across a tree that seemed to be shrouded in a veil. Edgar said, "Why is the inside of the tree moving. Look at it, you can see small things in the moonlight crawling on the veil."

The three got up close and soon discovered what was animating the tree when a couple of small spiders fell on Todd. He shook them off, realizing the entire tree was alive with them. He shouted, "Holy crap. This place is starting to creep me out. Look at this, the whole tree is like nothing but a spider colony."

The three of them backed away is disgust. Edgar said, "Come on, we have to be real careful where we're walking."

"We've got a lot of moonlight. Do you see that big willow tree? Let's go over there and plan what we'll do next. We might be able to climb up a little and see what's around here," said Larry.

The three nodded agreement and began to move cautiously toward the tree with a great deal less confidence than they had before entering the estate. When they arrived at Weird Willow, they heard a loud thrashing sound in the branches above, as they were studying how to climb it. Looking up, they could see nothing; so, they moved away from the trunk several feet, attempting to see.

Todd cried in shock, as a large bird dropping landed on his head. Scraping it off his scalp he exclaimed, "What. . . . What would be that big? Phew. Oh my goodness. It smells terrible. Ugh!" The other two recoiled from him and then the three looked up in wonder as Periwinkle flew away. They only caught a brief glimpse of the great bird, but it was enough to convince them to head in the direction of the wall and out of there quickly. They ran recklessly, finally coming to a large hedge that blocked their way to the wall.

They began to walk its length, hoping to find its end. They did just as a giant ape-like animal sprang from behind a tree, arms raised high, delivering a shrieking howl. The three stopped dead in their tracks and tried to step backwards. Losing their balance, they fell to the ground as Beau loomed over them, beating his chest in rage. Petrified, the three looked up in horror.

Crow witnessed this spectacle from behind a bush, a short distance away and then dashed in between Beau and his three fallen classmates. He raised his arms in front of Beau and shouted, "Stop. Quit. Go to you cave."

The three fallen adventurers were stunned and grateful for Crow's appearance. Beau bowed his head to Crow in compliance and withdrew. The three got up and tried to compose themselves.

Before they could speak, Crow angrily asked them, "What do you think you're doing here? What did you expect to find?"

Larry composed himself enough to speak, "We thought it would be like fun to see what's like really here. We didn't mean any harm."

Crow replied, "You're lucky I was up. If you wanted to see what was here, you could have asked me." Feeling stronger with a real sense of assertiveness, he continued, "If you want something, do it the right way. Your stupid comments about this place and me at school wouldn't even have made a difference. I would have let you see some of it."

Todd asked, "What was that? Was it some kind of ape?"

"It's a very rare creature that my father found and raised because it was abandoned by its parents."

Edgar asked, "Are you like going to call the cops on us?"

Crow paused for a minute before answering, "No, I don't think so, but you need to keep your mouths shut about what you saw here tonight. If you tell people about this, and my father finds out about it, he'll bring trespassing charges against you and your parents. He's a real dick about his privacy, so no, I won't tell. Are you going to mention this to anyone? I need an answer from each of you."

All three declared they would keep their mouths shut. Crow said, "OK, come on I'll show you a place where you can get over the wall. He led them to a utility shack, where he pulled a ladder out of the door and set it up against the wall. He said, "From the top of the wall here, you can lower yourself down and then drop a few feet to the other side."

They each climbed the ladder and dropped over the wall. Crow listened to them withdraw from the wall and hurry away, as his friendly white raven rejoined him on his shoulder. He walked to Beau's cottage and knocked on the door. Beau answered, "Come in, young Crow Master."

Crow sat down in front of him and said, "Thank you for doing that. You really scared them. I made them promise that they'd keep their mouths shut about everything. I hope they do, I wouldn't want to repeat the inspection from the state game and fish agency we had a few years back."

Beau, clothed in a red robe, replied, "I enjoyed the encounter. Although my performance was not quite Shakespearean, I think it got the job done. The only uncomfortable thing was completely disrobing. I was, frankly, a little embarrassed."

"I apologize for that, but I guess it had to be done."

"It's OK, there was something vaguely refreshing about running around *au naturel*. I suppose that's connected to my true nature."

"Do you ever get lonely Beau—I mean for your kind—whatever they are?"

"I honestly don't know what they'd be like. I was too young to remember when your father found me. Actually, I'm quite happy here. You all are very good to us, and everyone appreciates the care given. What about you, Crow? How are you feeling?"

"Mom came to school the other day and she brought Chuckles. Of course, she was a hit, but after tonight, I don't know how things will shake out. I hope those three we scared off keep their mouths shut about this place. They said they would, but you know how that goes."

Beau opined, "Don't worry about it. What will be, will be."

"You're right, but I'm curious about how they'll act tomorrow at school. Thanks again. I better get back to the house, otherwise the family might begin to wonder."

"Good night, young Crow Master."

❧ 10 ❧

Taking a Risk

On his way to school, a block before the campus, Crow saw Todd and Larry waiting by a hedgerow on the sidewalk. When they spotted him, they advanced to him quickly with real concern on their faces.

Todd spoke, "We need to talk. Edgar got busted last night. His mom caught him sneaking back into his room." Observing more students coming their way, Todd said, "Let's go to the park across from school and talk."

The three of them walked to a quiet place in the park. Crow asked, "Did he tell them what happened?"

Todd answered, "He tweeted me that he ducked out to meet a friend. He refused to say who we are and where we went, so they grounded him for the weekend. They wouldn't even let him go to school today."

Crow asked, "Do you think he'll keep to his story?"

Larry interjected, "Edgar wouldn't rat on anyone."

Crow said, "That may be true, but his parents will put two and two together and start asking you guys if you were with him."

Larry, directing his comments to Crow, said "You're right. Listen, if my parents start in on me, I'll tell them that we tried to get into your place, but we chickened out. Is that OK?"

Crow paused for a while and finally said, "I think I have a better idea. We have a half day today, right?"

Todd said, "Yea, the teachers are going to some conference."

"Right after school, I'll go to Edgar's house and tell his parents that I invited him to come, in secret, to my place and that I'd show him around without my parents knowing it. I'll tell him we both lost our nerve, when we saw them on the grounds late last night. Maybe that'll work."

Larry and Todd, simultaneously, said, "Wow, you'd do that for us?"

"I've got my reasons. Tweet him and tell him what's going on, so we're both on the same page."

Larry said, "Hold on, I think his parents took away his phone for the weekend."

Todd said, "That's OK, I know how to get to his room window without anybody seeing me. I'll let him know what's going on before you go to his home. We'll meet right here after school, then I'll go to his place to let him know what's going on, OK?" The three agreed.

After school Todd dashed off to Edgar's house and Larry and Crow waited for his return to the park. Crow spotted his shoulder companion in the sky and gave him a quick whistle. He landed on Crow's shoulder in short order. Crow stroked his breast.

Larry impressed with that move said, "That's so cool. Is he your personal pet?"

"Yea, I found him when he was young and kinda' raised him by myself."

"Is that why you call yourself Crow?"

"Yea, Cromwell totally sucks, but my mother and father insist on it. It pains me when our teachers call on me."

Larry commented, "This is the longest I've heard you talk."

"Yea, I guess I'm on the quiet side."

"You ought to speak up more often. You're an upright dude."

"Hey, I've heard some of the comments you guys have made about me and where I live."

Larry explained, "You shouldn't take stuff like that too seriously. It's the same BS we say to each other and everybody else."

Crow, surprised, said, "Really, why do you do that?"

"People take themselves too seriously. We can see it. We just let them know. Hold on, I see Todd running this way now."

Todd came up to them panting, catching his breath, he said, "OK, we're good to go. He hasn't said anything more to his parents, so you'll completely take his old man by surprise. Tell him just like you said, you know, that you like invited Edgar to sneak onto your estate. His house is only a couple streets from here."

Crow gave his shoulder companion a whistle and gentle shrug and he returned to the sky. Then he said, "Let's go. You guys stay close and I'll let you know what happens."

Todd said, "Don't worry, I know exactly where we can hide."

Crow approached the door with some trepidation, but he was resolved to do this thing—which was much more than covering for his family and M J Manor. He actually felt a need to protect Edgar. It surprised him, as he rang the front doorbell.

After a short wait, the door opened. Crow looked directly into Edgar's dad's eyes, inhaled deeply then forced himself to lie as effectively as he knew how. He saw before him a formidable large African American man whose muscular physique was crowned with close-cropped, curly, black hair and a beard to match.

Crow spoke before Edgar's father had a chance to ask who he was, "Sir, my name is Crow Monsterjunkie. Actually, it's Cromwell, but I start to gag when I say that name. I wanted to tell you that I'm responsible for Edgar's leaving home last night.

I dared him to come to our estate, where I was going to show him some of our animals. I heard he was being punished for what he did and I wanted to tell you what happened and that it was partially my fault. We spent some time together on the grounds, but there were too many people going back and forth, so we decided it was a bad idea, then he went home."

"Did your parents send you over here?"

"No sir, I came by myself. I thought it was the right thing to do."

Edgar's father asked, "Edgar has never mentioned you before. Are you one of his classmates?"

"Yes I am, sir."

The father's attitude relaxed and he said, "I hear a lot of strange things about your place. Are they true?"

"We keep some unusual animals, but they wouldn't harm anybody."

Edgar's father smiled and said, "So you don't like the name, Cromwell. I know what that's like. My parents named me, Aloysius. I despised it. For a while I thought they hated me and named me that to spite me. I finally got everybody to call me Al. OK, Crow, thanks for the heads up, I'll tell my wife. And, by the way, tell your buddies and anybody else. Your name is Crow. And if they don't like it, too bad. Got it?"

"Yes, I do. Thanks for your time, sir."

Crow left with a real sense of contentment as he walked toward the street. Before he reached the sidewalk, Todd and Larry sprung from behind a bush.

Todd shouted, "You were awesome."

Larry seconded him and said, "Hey, I think you pulled it off."

They both gave him high fives—something he'd never experienced before.

Crow, trying to be detached as well as he could under the circumstances, said "I guess I'll find out if Edgar's father decides to call my house. We'll see. Do you think Edgar's parents will let up on him?"

"I don't know," Todd answered, "They're hard to figure. One minute they can be tough and the next they'll let him off the hook. I guess we'll find out. Let's talk a little bit about last night. We were down by the ocean and we saw something that looked like a sea serpent. Do you know what that was?"

Crow answered, "A lot of strange stuff swims into the cove. We have a house there and we've seen some pretty odd things. I don't know if I know enough to give them names."

Larry asked, "What kind of a bird lives in that big willow tree?" He started laughing and said, "It took a dump on Todd's head. Phew! Man, that was really rank stuff."

Todd, grimacing said, "Thanks for mentioning that, a—hole."

Crow and Larry started laughing and Crow said, "Don't feel bad. She's tagged me a couple times, too. She's a giant bird from Indonesia."

Larry asked, "Will you still keep your offer open about coming to your place? We'd really like to see it."

"I'll see what I can do."

They reached the park area where they first met and Todd's cell phone rang. He shouted, "It's Edgar." He listened attentively to what Edgar was saying. He nodded his head and said, "Yeh, yeh, yeh, I'll tell him. See ya' after your captivity." Turning to Crow, he said, "Edgar told me to say thanks, but he is still grounded. He admitted to your version of what happened last night. At least he like got his cell phone back. He thinks the matter is over, so that's way cool."

Crow observed another of his classmates move to a tree about 30 yards from them and sit down by it. He was crying and it finally dawned on him that it was Mark Hodges, Winter's younger brother. Indigo had filled him in on Mark after their PTA meeting, where she met Winter, his older sister.

Crow pointed at Mark and asked, "Isn't that Mark Hodges?"

Larry said, "It looks like he's in a world 'a hurt."

"Let's see what the problem is," Crow said.

Todd speculated, "I've got a feeling I know what this is all about. Come on, let's check it out."

The three advanced to Mark and Crow asked him, "What happened, Mark?"

Mark, wiping the blood from his nose, said, "I was jumped by these guys from another class. They said some nasty things about my sister and then started pushing me around. I'm not very big and I guess they thought I was an easy target. They called her a 'stupid dyke.' It really made me mad. I took a swing at the guy who said that and then they ganged up on me."

Todd asked him, "Did you catch any names?"

Mark answered, "There were three of them, but there was one guy the other two seemed to listen to more, like some kind of leader. It sounded like 'Wruth.'"

Todd said, "That must be Rutherford J Grimes III, called 'Ruth' like the first syllable of Rutherford. I'll give you a very brief history. His grandparents—crooks, some say—made their money on Wall Street and decided to become country gentry in New England—what my mom would call the *nouveau riche*, or new rich. He talks like he has a small turd under his nose. 'Ruth' builds up his phony image at other people's expense. His mother and father inherited all of grand-daddy's loot and pretend to be self-important moral authorities. I guess some people are impressed by their showy BS, but not my folks."

Larry volunteered to Mark, "Let me get you some wet paper towels out of the bathroom so you can clean up. I'll be right back."

Todd continued, "I overheard Ruth talking to his brown-nosing buddies and he was saying it wasn't right to have 'fags' and 'lezzies' mixed in with 'normal' folks—like he's a perfectly normal specimen. It looks like he targeted your sister, as an example, which is ridicu lous, because I've seen her around guys quite a bit. If you don't mind me saying so, I think she's hot. He probably made a snap judgment based on her clothes. One of his group probably identified you as her brother, hence your current condition."

Mark asked, "Does this mean they'll be on my case from now on?"

"I don't know, maybe, maybe not. It's hard to predict with that crew."

Larry returned with some wet paper towels and Mark started to clean up. Crow helped him straighten himself up and said, "I'll walk with you a bit. Your place is probably before M J Manor. We can talk."

Todd said, "We're out of here." Then to Crow, "See ya' Monday. Try not to be a dick head in class."

Crow smiled at his remark and said, "OK, ass wipe."

Todd laughed, "Now you're learning."

Larry said, "Check with your father about us visiting."

Crow replied, "I'll see what my old man has to say about it. Don't hold your breath. I just hope Edgar's father didn't call our house." Crow watched them walk away and experienced a sense that had never touched him before—a real feeling of self-confidence. He had never referred to Dr. Monsterjunkie as his 'old man' and it gratified him deeply to have said it. He had improvised the entire day, took a serious risk and he genuinely liked the outcome—but now he had two new concerns, Mark Hodges and Rutherford J Grimes III. He thought, *What if I called him 'Ruth,' using the girl's pronunciation—or even Ruthy. Would he try to hit me? Would Todd and the other two back me up? Interesting thought.*

He turned to Mark as the two walked silently to Mark's house and he finally broke the silence and asked, "How are you feeling? You look OK, you stopped the nosebleed."

"Thanks, I'm really glad you guys showed up. Do you think I should tell my dad about what happened?"

Crow thought a bit and said, "Run it by your sister first. She'll help you figure it out. I'll tell Indigo and she'll call her, too and then you can decide."

They arrived in front of Mark's house and he turned to Crow with a lost look on his face and said. "This stuff happened to my sister in the last town we lived in. It's like it followed us. Nobody stood up for us, except my dad. Thanks for being here today. Crow was moved by his situation and said, "This is a problem that can be solved. You're not alone, OK?"

They parted company and Crow walked home with many things on his mind.

✂ 11 ✂

Reservations Made

Crow saw Indigo lounging on the front porch talking on her 'smart'er than human' phone. She gestured that he stick around, so he sat down beside her. He overheard her saying that she'd ask her parents if Winter could spend the night. He also heard she'd talk with her about Mark. She put her phone in her pocket and turned to Crow.

"I was wandering, what happened to Mark?" she asked.

"Do you know a rambunctious boy named Rutherford J Grimes III?"

"I know of him, he's not in any of my classes, but I understand he's in one of Winter's. She just told me he was the one responsible for Mark getting bullied—even beat up. I know quite a few people in the school, but he's one of those people I prefer avoiding just based on his reputation. I've heard he's snobby, pushy and an average student—with a somewhat nasty nature and his friends are just like him. I guess they hold sway over some—you know, the money status types—but none of my friends and acquaintances have anything to do with them."

Crow said, "It was he and two of his friends that beat Mark up."

Indigo asked, "How'd you get mixed up in all of this?"

"I was with a couple of guys from my class and we spotted him in the park. He was pretty messed up, so we cleaned him up and I walked home with him."

"I talked to Winter about it and she really appreciates what you did. Mark feels a connection to something now. Who were the other guys with you?"

"Todd and Larry, they're both in my class. We were out of school and so we hooked-up in the park across the street."

"Are they your friends?"

"Kinda', we've done a few things together."

"That's way cool."

"Listen Indy, can you go to bat for me on something, especially with mom. You know how I hate the name Crom. I don't even want to say the full name. Ask mom to call me Crow. Tell her how simple it could be going from Crom to Crow—just a change of one letter. I think if mom goes along with it, dad will probably follow suit. OK?"

"You're funny. All right, I'll add it to the things I want from her. I want to bring a new friend here for an overnighter—something I've never done. I had a feeling I would meet someone like her when I went to that PTA meeting with Mom."

Crow, concerned about the consequences of bringing outsiders asked, "How much of this place are you going to show her and how much will Mom and Dad let you?"

"Good questions, my answer is, I plan to push the envelope. I'm tired of all this secrecy and all the stupid rumors that we're harboring 'monsters.' It's time to be honest about the extraordinary animals of nature we interact with."

Crow, thinking of Edgar, Todd and Larry, said, "Yeh, I agree with you totally. I wouldn't mind having people over myself."

"Good, I think the best way to handle this is for me to talk to her now. I don't want to bring this up over our formal dinner tonight, so I'll find her right now. I won't forget to ask about the name thing. I know from experience that Dad will agree with just about anything she asks."

"Thanks Indy, you're a standup babe."

She laughed and asked, "What did you just call me? As a matter of fact, what happened to you today? You're different, I can tell."

"Oh, I don't know, I just feel like experimenting with words. What I said sounded right to me."

"OK, but this 'standup babe' has things to do, I'll see you later."

Indigo knocked on Pandora's bedroom door and she invited her daughter in. Indigo inhaled her mother's perfumes of jasmine and lavender, a scent of which she never tired. Pandora arose from her vanity chair and swirled around to greet Indigo. She was clothed in a formal evening gown, another mixture of black and grays that clung to her contours. She said, "Good evening Indy, what brings you here?"

"I wanted to talk to you about a few things before dinner. When we were at the PTA meeting, I met a very interesting person and I want to invite her here for a sleepover."

"I'm not surprised, your intuition has served you well. Do you have confidence she can handle the overwhelming experience of the estate?"

"Yes, I do."

Pandora thoughtfully assessed the situation and said, "I've thought about opening up this sanctuary to more people, but most of the time my reservations win out and I simply dismiss it. Why do you consider—Winter, that's her name, right?—a good candidate?"

Indigo replied, "I know we consider ourselves normal and I appreciate the fact that 'normal' is an imprecise word, but I often feel like a foreigner. Secrecy is really not a part of my personality. I play the game of being discreet very well, especially at school, but it's not me. I see Winter as an outsider and I can be honest with her, she's smart, artistic, and, in a short time, we've become friends. What this all boils down to is this—I want you to trust me with Winter. I believe that after she's been here, she'll respect us and our special world—the one that you and Dad, Elizabeth and Ernest, Isabella and Conrad created for our family—regardless of what she sees."

Pandora studied her and replied, "I respect what you've just said and your judgments about people are usually very accurate. You have my permission to bring her for the overnighter. I think I can convince your father and I will trust you to do the right thing with her introduction. When would you like her to come?"

"Tomorrow night. For dinner too, if that's all right. Mother, I can't thank you enough. You have no idea how much I appreciate this. There's one more thing that Crow asked me to ask you. It's the Cromwell issue. I noticed a real change in behavior with him today. He called me a 'stand up babe,' and I laughed. I've never heard him say anything like that before. I actually think he's found some friends, I think he's absorbing their lingo. But he really wants to be called Crow. I think it's that bird he loves, but it's also him locking on to an identity. Please run that by Father also, I know it means a lot to him, OK?"

Pandora, with obvious pride for her daughter beamed, "I'm so proud of you. You are so poised, articulate and beautiful. We couldn't be happier with you." She walked over to her and embraced her. "You'd best get ready for dinner."

Indigo returned to her room and called Winter and nearly shouted, "We're on for tomorrow night. Is that OK? I'm so excited, but I need to tell you a few things. I've kinda' hinted at some of the strange beings that live here, but now I need to tell you what to expect."

Winter, gushing with excitement said, "Go ahead. I can't wait. This is so cool."

"OK, we'll have dinner around 7:00, but have your dad drop you off around 6:00, so you'll have time to settle in. Our dinners are a little on the formal side, but we don't expect our guests, as few as they are, to dress up."

"Don't worry about it. I have some dress up connects. I'll pack a nice gown. Listen, this is important. Can I bring my ISketch? I know how you guys are about your privacy and I promise I won't share sketches with anybody you don't approve of, OK?"

"Sure, bring it with you. We'll figure out what to do with your sketches later. Two people you'll see at dinner are Betty and Frances. They are pituitary giants who came from the circus. My father rescued them when they were very young. If we have time later, they'll tell you their story. The big shocker of the evening will be your encounter with a legendary entity, still largely hidden from worldview."

"Oh, wow. My head is buzzing with possibilities. It'll be so cool to meet your parents and brother, as well as seeing everything."

Indigo continued, "Later in the evening, I want to take you to our beach house. The ocean is really beautiful in the cove. A lot of bioluminescent fish are visible in the depths and, if we're lucky, we'll see something really special. It's a special secret."

Winter asked, "How do you keep a place like yours running? It's really a big property. Do you have servants?"

"Not in the classic sense of servants; Betty and Frances do a lot, along with that other special being I talked about and we have a Masters college student along with others. Besides, all of us chip in taking care of our animal friends, and making sure the place runs smoothly. I haven't thought of us as a team before, but that's pretty much what we are. Tomorrow night, Betty will cook and Frances will help her serve, but sometimes I help mom with some meals, too."

"I'm thrilled you invited me. See ya' tomorrow evening."

❧ 12 ❧

Meet the Family

E d Hodges dropped Winter at the front gate. The monumental front gate was constructed from the same stone as the surrounding estate wall with two wrought iron gates, separating the wall on either side and soaring over the iron to form a towering edifice with 'Monsterjunkie' in the center. She pressed the intercom button and, after a short pause, the gate opened with an almost eerie, ancient squeak. Winter waved goodbye to her dad, as he drove away.

She walked down a manicured approach to the front door. Over the front double door entrance was an arched, sculpted collection that contained impressions of many rare and mythical animals. She smiled at the intricacy of the detail of each creature: a unicorn, a gorilla, an ice age mammoth and an elephant bird. She had not studied all of them when the door opened and Indigo came out to welcome her.

Indigo hugged her and said, "I'm so glad you could come."

"This bas-relief is awesome. Who did this?

"Cool, I didn't even know that's what you call it. Our grandfather Conrad commissioned the work when he built this place and grandmother Isabella selected the creatures she wanted in it. They passed away before I was born, but I do wish I'd known them. They emigrated from Germany back in the early 20th century. Fortunately, I was able to briefly know my Grandfather Ernest and Grandmother Elizabeth. But Conrad was just like my father, Talon, a great explorer and animal lover. Father learned all of his skills with animals from his renowned parents and grandparents and he inherited that amazing ability to connect in rare situations. Grandfather Ernest educated him in all the specifics. Come on, let's go in."

They entered the grand foyer, family oil paintings and landscape paintings hung on the vaulted walls. Huge sculpted animals in granite, bronze and wood were interspersed in niches and on elegant risers along the corridor leading to the great room and library with a grand piano. There were no mounted trophy animal heads or stuffed animals anywhere in the home; they only had sculptures representing various animals.

In the great room, Indigo led Winter over to the Medieval stone carved fireplace. Above, looking down, were the portraits of Isabella and Conrad—benign, kind faces, the artist had captured their warmth and humanity in what could only be described as a distinguished painting.

Winter caught the quality of their countenances and said, "You can tell what kind of people they were just by their portraits. What courage they had to venture half way around the world to a place like New England."

Indigo shared, "I wish I'd known them. In a way, I kinda' do, through Dad's stories of them and Mom's recollections. Fortunately, I did know my grandparents, Ernest and Elizabeth. Come on, we'll get you settled in one of our guest rooms, close to my room. Mother and Father are out now and the rest of our folks are doing other things.

She led Winter to another wing on the second floor of the Manor where her bedroom, as well as a couple of guest rooms, were located. As they walked down the hall, Indigo leaned over and picked up what Winter thought was a stuffed animal.

"This is Stormy," as Indigo scratched her head.

"I thought it was a stuffed animal, what is it?"

"It's a long-haired rabbit, I think they are called Angora rabbits, he loves to be held."

"How come you named him Stormy?" Winter queried.

"He's so harmless, it's just funny." said Indigo.

They continued and Winter exclaimed, as she entered her room and opened her suitcase on her bed, "This is really neat. Oh my, look at the view you get from this window. The grounds are so lush and that willow out there is amazing. Wow, hold on a minute. I see Crow out there throwing a ball to a dog—wait, is that a dog? I've never seen anything like *that* before."

"Oh, he must be playing with Chico. Chico is a chupacabra. My father found him in Mexico. There was a lot of dispute about whether they existed or not, but we have living proof."

Winter asked, "Will your father ever make his find public?"

"Perhaps some day, but I do know he's working with a scientific group to determine exactly what kind of animal it is. Sometimes, Chico sure acts like a dog."

Looking at her open suitcase, Indigo said, "I see you brought your ISketch. Any time you get the urge to start penciling, just let me know. You'll have plenty of material to work with here."

Winter pulled a dress, a deep maroon sheath, from her suitcase and held it in front of her, "Will this do?"

"It's great, I love that color. It looks like one of the deep red wines Father gets from Italy and California. If I have a chance, I'll show you his wine cellar. I guess Isabella and Conrad brought the European wine tradition to the US. Do you want some time before dinner?"

"Yeah, I'd like to sketch that willow tree out there while the light is still good."

"Great, I'll stop by when we need to get ready for dinner. See ya' then."

Winter sat by the picture window and began to frame the initial impressions of the willow with surrounding lush vegetation. She kept looking and sketching and then, after a bit, she looked up and saw Periwinkle glide to the interior of Weird Willow. Her mouth opened and, as she gasped, she thought, *"Oh my goodness. This place is too amazing."*

Indigo and Winter descended the ornate spiral staircase in the library and walked slowly down the hallway, allowing Winter to absorb the beauty of the structure and its art treasures. "This spiral stair was commissioned by Conrad with a wood craftsman from the old country. The inlay, taking advantage of the grain direction, produced a unique addition, coupled with the carved ebony lion heads as balustrades," Indigo said.

"The spiral staircase is way cool," observed Winter.

They arrived at the entrance of the dining room and Winter preceded her inside. Pandora, Talon and Crow were standing by a serving counter. Talon poured a fine California Syrah into cobalt blue and cranberry red Val St. Lambert wine glasses from a facetted crystal Waterford carafe for himself and Pandora.

Indigo approached her father and said, "Dr. Monsterjunkie, let me introduce you to my friend, artiste extraordinaire, Ms. Winter Hodges."

Talon responded with his usual formal courtesy and, in European fashion, kissed her hand and said, "Welcome to M J Manor. I hope you enjoy your stay."

"Thank you so much for inviting me."

Pandora advanced to her and shook hands, "Indy has said so many nice things about you. I'm glad you can stay with us."

Crow approached her and before he could say anything, she embraced him and said, "I can't thank you enough for what you and your friends did for my brother, Mark. You guys were so cool."

Crow slightly embarrassed, but somewhat pleased by her hug, minimized his help, "We just happened to be in the right place at the right time. How's he doing?

"I think he's OK now, but he's concerned about it happening again."

They were interrupted by the arrival of Frances and Betty, the twins that Indigo had briefed Winter about. The two brought several items to the dining table and carefully adjusted the place settings. They were each nearly eight feet tall, but possessed mostly normal features—handsome actually—except for their larger heads, which were not in any way grotesque. Winter was struck by their extraordinary size, but more so by their serene calm, not only reflected on their faces, but also in the way they carried themselves with their careful, smooth, but quietly assertive gestures. When the two came over to the group, Indigo introduced them and each carefully extended her hand in a surprisingly gentle and supple handshake.

Frances said to Talon, "Beau is running behind a little bit; he's having trouble with his tuxedo cummerbund."

Talon responded, "Tell him not to worry. We're not in a rush. We'll have dinner, after we've had time to chat with everyone. Please bring your glasses, let's take our seats.

The dining room table was an impressive European piece brought from Bavaria by Conrad when they came to America. Two elegant old world candelabras illuminated the table and surrounding area. Talon seated himself at the head of the table after he had seated Pandora to his right. Crow sat by his mother, while Indigo and Winter seated themselves opposite. Winter noticed that two chairs on her side of the table and the two across from them had no place settings—but, oddly, there was one at the other end of the table.

Her puzzle was soon solved as Talon stood and greeted Beauregard when he entered the room. All eyes turned to Beau as he greeted the group in a deep, melodious voice, "Good evening to you all," and as his eyes turned to Winter, he said, "and also to our very special guest, Ms. Hodges."

Winter's jaw dropped in disbelief, but she remembered what Indigo said about surprises. She composed herself immediately, enough to get up and extend her hand to an articulate bigfoot—an almost impossible concept, but a living reality she was about to touch. She grasped his hand and again, his grip, like Betty and Frances', was also surprisingly soft to the touch. Composing herself, she said, "From this day on, I'll always believe anything is possible.

Can I ask you some questions?" The Monsterjunkie family nodded their gratified approval to each other.

Beau gallantly responded, "It's my great pleasure to answer questions and, I hope, modestly, to entertain you with my replies."

As she was about to speak to Beau, he anticipated her question and said, "Let me briefly explain my history and, I think, that will help you understand me. Dr. Monsterjunkie and his adventuresome pilot, Race, rescued me at a very young age. I have no idea how old I actually was, but I do recall my parents. I honestly don't know why I was abandoned. When I saw Race's hydroplane swoop down from the sky, it was like some deity descending from Olympus—although I would not have thought of that simile at the time.

"They loaded me in that sky machine and, as we flew south from the great North Country, I began to articulate words from our ancient language. You see what you call 'Bigfoot' are actually an intelligent primate species with language ability. There are numerous names for our kind and the others like us that inhabit this world. Most of us are masters of invisibility and we congregate infrequently in very private locations. We are extremely resilient and can survive what you would characterize as great hardship—which to us is simply day-to-day life."

Winter, with amazement, interjected, "You speak so well. I'm just awestruck."

Beau continued, "Thank you. You're very kind. Master Talon actually has made a very short dictionary of the childhood words that I knew at the time of my rescue. He also video recorded some of my speech and the accompanying gestures."

Talon interrupted him saying, "Beauregard mastered English in record time. Through sign language, he was able to understand and communicate and shortly gained the verbal aspect of our language. Now, he could easily be on the English faculty at Maine College. In fact that group's prestige would improve considerably with his inclusion, but that's beside the point. The real truth is that his love of poetry and his ability to create it are very impressive. Sorry to interrupt, please continue."

Crow gestured to his father that he wished to speak. Talon acknowledged him saying, "Do you wish to say something, Cromwell?" Then, after a pause, "Crow."

Crow beamed from ear to ear, smiled gratefully at his sister and mother and said, "Beau wrote a poem about me and I'd like him to recite it." He turned to Beau and asked, "Is that OK with you?"

"Of course."

No one, other than Crow and Beau, at the table had ever heard it before, and Indigo commented immediately, "Crow, that's really you." Turning to Beau she said, "That was brilliant," then to Crow, "Do you think the last lines are true about you?"

Answering very coyly, he simply said, "We'll see."

Indigo, not accepting his coolness, said, "Aren't you going to tell us about your new friends?"

Not changing his demeanor, he replied, "Yesterday was the first time we had any real talks, but so far so good."

Winter chimed in, "The three of you showed your real character when you helped my brother. My family will always appreciate it."

Winter turned to Beau and asked, "Are you happy with your life here? Do you ever miss just being out on your own?"

"No, I realize the impossibility of entering into the world out here. In some ways I'm like Master Talon. I enjoy my privacy and I love exploring the realities of this world, which are so very different from whence I came. I write extensively and maybe some day, when conditions are right, I'll release that to the world, along with some poems that I deem suitable for publication."

Pandora commented to Winter, "As you have probably noticed, our privacy is, in part, our strategy to keep safe the rare and wonderful animals we've chosen to protect. However, as the world changes, so must we. We intend to open our estate to more people, but, for obvious reasons, we must do this cautiously. We all agree on that point and, I might add, that we are impressed with how you're handling this."

Winter replied, "It looks like you've chosen me to be one of those people and I can't begin to tell you how much I appreciate this evening."

Frances interrupted the group, as she announced dinner was about to be served. Soon, Betty, who began serving a vegetable soup, helped her distribute the bowls. Everyone grew silent for a while, as they savored the light, delicately seasoned soup that Betty had prepared from her vegetable garden.

Winter had just finished her soup course, when she experienced a tugging at her right arm. She looked down in surprise as a pygmy elephant wrapped its small trunk around her arm and stared at her longingly.

She exclaimed, "Oh my goodness, a… a miniature elephant."

Talon corrected her, "It's actually a pygmy elephant from Borneo. We call him 'Thunder.' Indigo is the one who named him; she liked the sound of it and he responded to the name immediately."

Winter knelt and embraced him, saying, "He acts like he's hungry, may I feed him some cold vegetables from the table?"

Talon said, "Of course, please do, we feed him bites all the time. A lot of his behaviors are just like a dog's. Actually, he is somewhat like a dog."

Winter began to feed him cherry tomatoes and carrot chunks, as he squeaked in appreciation, wagging his tail in delight. She returned to her seat, as the main course was served, which was a pasta dish, with a variety of cheeses and mixed vegetables."

Winter asked Talon, "Dr. Monsterjunkie, are you all vegetarians?"

"Yes, we prefer naturally grown fruits, vegetables, tubers and natural uncooked foods."

"I do too. My dad still eats fish, but very little red meat," added Winter.

Talon noted, "Pandora thought your father brought up some good points about bullying at the PTA meeting she and Indigo attended. What do you think your father will do about the incident with your brother?"

"He plans to see the principal Monday. That's what he did when I was harassed at my other school. It gave me some relief, but it didn't solve the problem. I hope the people who hurt my brother will be punished, but I'm realistic enough to know it will be my brother's word against three others."

Indigo interjected, "The person who provoked that scene was Rutherford J Grimes III. We've talked about him before. He has a little clique that likes to show off their delusional social position. I guess there are some folks in our community that fall for their phony game. Most of the people I know think he's a creep."

Crow spoke up, "Todd's mom and dad called his family, *nouveau . . . nouveau* ."

Talon finished it for him, ". . .*riche*, which means newly rich and it also implies pretension—which is a fancy word for showy claims to status—because of the things your money buys."

Crow said, "That's kinda what Todd said."

Talon asked, "Is Todd one of your new friends?"

"I believe so."

Indigo asked, "Father, why do you think people need to be pretentious, or try to make themselves superior to folks who are different from them?"

Talon explained, "It's probably a combination of several human behaviors, which are not the best parts of humanity. To be suspicious of strangers is a common reflex, among most cultures. I've encountered it many times in my travels. There is a word, ethnocentrism, which means your tribe, community, or even a nation - because of your strong connection to it, creates a feeling of—'We're-better-than-you.'

Pandora asked, "Isn't Conrad's emigration to the United States a perfect example of this?"

"Absolutely, Conrad understood it and feared its consequences. In his youth, he lost his oldest brother in the Franco Prussian war and, after that, he saw the rise of nationalist Europe, where entire nations carried their fear of each other and their will to try to make themselves superior to their neighbors to dreadful violent ends, including two world wars.

"He realized where this was all heading very early, and then began transferring his assets to this country—and eventually Isabella and himself to America before World War One began. He believed this country would free him from the terrors of European nationalism. That was largely true, but we still see minor versions of it in our communities, where it's based on money, status, race or ideology."

Beau supported that position saying, "One of the reasons we, meaning our kind, 'bigfoot' animals and others, live in nature's shadows is because we are so different—and, therefore, feared by many. We are the true 'strangers,' more so than any others. In many places of the world, some hunt us, not even trying to capture us for their amusement. They would prefer to kill us with their weapons and display us as stuffed trophies in their homes or museums. Many of the hidden or frightened things of the world remain so, because of the 'We're-better-than-you' mentality that oppresses them. You have to look no further than the victims of bullying as examples. But as a matter of fact, 'Race,' that's his nickname, I believe his name is Randall, he is Master Talon's adventuresome pilot, was instrumental in helping to save me."

After completing the main course, Betty and Frances served a lemon sorbet for dessert. Conversation turned to lighter subjects like school projects and Talon's recollections of his many adventures with animals around the world. At the conclusion of dinner, Beau suggested that everybody retire to the library to play Scrabble and other word games, which, he claimed, helped inspire his poetry.

As everybody began to move to the library, Talon held Crow back so he could talk with him.

Talon asked, "Betty and Frances reported seeing tracks on the estate grounds and other evidence that several people had been here recently. Do you know anything about this?"

Crow gulped and inhaled deeply and decided to tell essentially what he told Edgar's father with one important modification, "Sir, Todd and two others, Edgar and Larry came onto our property on a dare. When I found out what they were doing, I made them get out of here. His mom and dad caught Edgar, while he tried to sneak back into his house. When I found out about the discovery, I went to his home and told his dad what happened. I didn't want to hide anything and I thought they'd ease up on Edgar, if I told them what really happened. Sir, when they came in here they didn't hurt anything. They wouldn't do anything like that."

Talon studied him and then a smile crossed his countenance as he asked, "Do they call you Crow?"

"Yes, they do."

"I learned from your mother how important that is and, if that is what you really desire, that's the way it will be. Do you have enough confidence in your friends, that you could bring them here for a visit, in much the same way Indigo did for Winter?"

"Sir, our friendship is recent, but I know they really want to see this place."

Talon said, "Feel them out a little bit and emphasize the importance of how they share information about this place. People like Rutherford J Grimes III are not the kind of folks we want visiting our home. Do you understand?"

"Yes sir, they would be cool about that."

"Crow, after you talk to them about coming here, let me know what you think and we'll take it from there, OK?"

"Thanks, Father."

"Good, you can join the others in the library, but I have some work to complete for my next trip."

Crow gave him a hug and and said, "Good night, this means a lot to me. Thanks."

"I know it does, son. Good night."

∞ 13 ∞

Cottage Tales

After games in the library, everyone retired for the evening. Indigo and Winter returned to the bedroom wing. Indigo said, "Change into comfortable clothes, I want to show you some other things. I'll do the same."

"Awesome, it'll take me just a few minutes."

Later Indigo returned and signaled Winter to join her. The two walked to the end of the wing and down a stairs to a door that allowed them to exit the main house.

Indigo closed the exit door to the gardens very quietly, locking it with her key. She said, "We'll go by Betty and Frances's cottage. If they're still up, we'll talk. Their place has a quaint European, Hansel and Gretel feel to it, except that my father did all of the furniture in a size that fits their bodies."

Under a full moon, they passed through a manicured garden area with many rare plants. Winter noticed that a large rose garden reflected only dark flowers and asked, "Do you have other roses besides black ones?"

"Yes, but these were specially bred by my great grandfather, my grandfather Ernest loved them and we've kept them flourishing through the years. We call Betty and Frances's place Black Rose Cottage. Conrad had the street Black Rose Parkway named after this garden. You'd be surprised to see how beautiful they look in an arrangement with other flowers. Betty loves arranging them and she constantly surprises us with her creations. Father said that Conrad bred them because that's what he said would be the color of the times in Europe that followed their coming to America."

"Was your grandfather Conrad some kind of a prophet?"

"I don't know about prophet, but he sure got the 20th century right. It was black with hatred and evil. Do you see the cottage ahead? There's a light on, they're probably up, I'll give them a knock."

The door opened and the stature of Betty filled the enlarged doorway. She smiled at the two girls and invited them in.

Winter said, "Thank you for a wonderful meal. That was truly special."

"My pleasure, dear, it was nice to have a guest, which doesn't happen often. Please come in."

Winter and Indigo passed through the kitchen and into their living room, where they were seated on a couch opposite two large easy chairs, each with a specially designed ottoman. Frances entered the room, and reclined in one of their two favorite resting places, while a fire crackled in the fireplace.

As Frances joined the group, Winter asked, "How did the two of you come to this manor?"

Betty responded, "May I compliment you on your lovely burgundy dress, your manners are quite proper. It's a long story, dear, and much of it has been explained to us by Master Talon, because we were very young when it happened." A deep sadness settled over her countenance as she explained, "It looks like we were sold to a circus, what used to be called a 'freak show.' I do remember my mother turning away in shame when she gave us away. I know money was exchanged, then she just walked away and never looked back.

We never knew our father. Even when mother kept us for a while, we knew something wasn't right and, after some people talked to her, for some reason, she didn't want us any more. I remember very little about where we lived. It's funny I can still recall the melody of a child's lullaby—just vaguely—I don't know why."

Frances added, "We are what's called pituitary giants; something happened to that gland in our brains that resulted in our size. Being identical twins, we both had the same rare condition."

Betty continued, "We were born in some eastern European country near Germany. We were only three or four years old, when our mother gave us away, but already we were very big. The show manager used to dress us up in costumes, like giant babies. He made us wear bonnets that made our heads look even larger and we had to do ridiculous skits, so we could make the people who paid to see us laugh at us. I'm not sure of the time, but I think we did this for four or five years.

We were part of a group: a dwarf, who was old with a long beard; a man they called Pinhead, with an unusually tiny skull; and, an older woman with a beard. We all performed skits. The one thing that hurt the most was when children our age would make up nasty things to say, rhymes and such, while pointing fingers at us. I guess after awhile we got used to it, but Frances and I always dreamed we'd have a better life.

We knew we had good minds in strange bodies and we did what we could to learn. The bearded lady used to help us with basic literacy. She took some time teaching us reading and writing. At the

81

end of the day at least, in the dark nights of loneliness, we had each other and, I think, that kept us going."

Frances continued, "When Master Talon was young, he returned to Germany to see where his family was raised. It happened the circus was travelling through that part of Germany. Master Talon, as you know, always looks for the exceptional things of the world. On a whim, he decided to see the freak show. He was shocked at what he saw.

He came up to us and began to ask questions. We saw that he was becoming very upset when he discovered what was happening to us."

Betty added, "He disappeared for a bit and came back with the manager of the circus. Before that, we both could hear Master Talon yelling at him, forcefully suggesting what he was doing to us was against German child abuse laws. Well, anyway to make a long story short, he took us away from that place and brought us to a beautiful chalet.

"For several days, we ate good food and wore real clothes. It took about a week for him to finish the paperwork; but after that, we all boarded a train to Hamburg, not far from France and proceeded to Rotterdam where we took a big ocean liner to the United States.

"It was as if we were living a dream. We were happy and excited. On the ocean voyage, Master Talon began to teach us English and how to write. When we came here and met Lady Pandora, we thought we were in heaven."

Frances said, "Our new life here became an adventure. And, here we are today living in the midst of this incredible garden world."

Winter, wiping tears from her eyes, composed herself and said, "That's the most heart-felt story I've ever heard, both of you are simply wonderful."

"I know our life here has been good, that's certain," Betty affirmed.

Winter asked, "Do you ever have a chance to get out and see some of the countryside?"

Frances answered, "Once in awhile, Master Talon and the family take us on a boat ride or a drive up the coast, but neither of us are very public people and the family is careful about who sees us. We feel protected here."

Winter asked, "Would you allow me to sketch you tomorrow? I'd be very honored if you let me do drawings of you."

"If it's all right with Master Talon or Lady Pandora, it would be nice. What would you do with the sketches?" asked Frances.

"I'd keep them in my sketchbook or give them to Pandora, I'd never make them public. I mostly want to keep them to remember this night."

Winter asked, "I noticed you used the words 'Master' and 'Lady.' Aren't those somewhat formal?"

Betty answered, "I've not considered it. It's formal and we know Beauregard uses them also. Certainly, neither Lady Pandora nor Master Talon has ever insisted we use those words, I think they just slip out because we respect them so much and it is our way of honoring them."

Indigo, who had remained silent for a while, spoke, "Both of my parents are formal people, but they relax a lot too. In some ways this place looks more like something you'd find in Europe than the US, but I think that's starting to change. Your presence here tonight, Winter, is probably part of it."

Winter asked, "What do you do when you need medical help, you know basic health care?"

Frances answered, "Conrad saw what was happening in Germany before World War Two, and he talked his young German doctor friend, Dr. Engelhard Arzneimittel, into emigrating to the United States. He and his wife, Ana, are Jewish. Master Conrad always seemed to know what was going to happen in Europe, so he helped him set up his practice in Bar Harbor. They passed their practice on to their son, Dr. Arnold. He and his wife, Eva, come here regularly, mostly to visit, but also to give us all check ups."

"Has that doctor ever treated Beau?"

"No, Master Talon takes care of that. Beau is probably the healthiest person in M J Manor. I remember Master Talon saying Beau's immune system and physical endurance are to be envied. He takes Beau's lab work to a special place where they study it. That's all I know," said Frances.

"You love your work here, don't you?" asked Winter.

Betty responded, "Yes, we do. This place is a treasure of nature, we are so fortunate. We help to keep the grounds beautiful and the things that Master Talon brings are always remarkable. Like I said, this is like living a fantasy."

Indigo, sensing that both were tired, said, "I think we ought to be going now. Thank you for inviting us in."

Winter said good night and stepped over to Betty and embraced her, "You both are wonderful. Thank you for sharing your amazing story." She reached over to Frances and did the same. The twins saw them to the door and waved to them as they disappeared into the depths of the estate.

14

Surprise at Mystic Cove

They continued their path through the estate, this time heading for Mystic Cove. The full moon illuminated the way and the silhouette of the trees and the distant splash on the shore created a sense of anticipation that grew in Winter and Indigo.

Winter asked, "Why won't you tell me anything about this cove?"

"I think it's something you need to see for yourself, and when we're done here, it will probably still be a mystery to both of us. You'll see."

They arrived at the summer boathouse, removed a basket from just inside the door and then moved to the dock area, where they stood looking at the rippling water in the cove. The full moon created a stunning cool blue appearance for the entire area as fog was developing in the distance, where the cove opened to the Atlantic.

Indigo stared in that direction and then smiled in anticipation. "Be prepared, brace yourself for another special sight."

The fog had drifted further into the cove, but there was still enough visibility to see something gracefully moving towards them. As it slinked secretively closer to the dock, it soon became obvious to Winter that she was probably the only 'outsider' to witness the arrival of a colossal sea monster or serpent to M J Manor. She stood silently, as the great snake-like creature slowly glided to the dock area where they were standing.

Indigo said, "Here she comes."

Winter asked, "Is this what I think it is?"

"If you mean a sea serpent, then you're right."

Indigo removed two large yellow squashes from her basket and held them, one in each hand with her arms extended. The serpent came directly in front of her and by its motion, elevated partially out of the water to an impressive height. The sea serpent, actually a *Cadborosaurus willsi*, had a nickname, Water Horse. Her head appeared much like a horse's, but she has mysterious red-golden eyes, which, for some reason, appeared sad.

Motioning towards the serpent, Indigo said, "Meet Sybil, the sea serpent, she's been our friend for over 15 years, now."

When Sybil lowered herself to Indigo's level, the two could see the extraordinary features of her face, the eyes were much like snake eyes and the mouth was etched in a perpetual smile-like twist. The coloring of the body was lighter mottled green scales on top of a darker shade, almost black, on the underside. She was clearly used to Indigo, as Indigo extended one of the squashes to her, she confident-ly plucked it from her hand and swallowed it whole. She briefly scrutinized Winter, returned her gaze to Indigo, watching Indigo pass the second squash to Winter."

"Would you like to feed her?"

Winter accepted th squash, faking calm, "Sure, why not?"

She held the squash and cautiously extended it to Sybil. The great sea serpent gently plucked that one away, also. As if in a celebratory dance, she swam around the cove and, then, meandered out to sea.

"Oh my goodness. What planet are we on? I simply don't have words for this." She spontaneously embraced Indigo and kissed her.

Catching herself in the act— "I'm sorry, maybe that was too forward."

Quickly, Indigo responded, "No, it's delightful. You just honestly showed your joy. Please don't apologize. " She went over and embraced her again.

Indigo said, "You see, that felt good too."

Winter frowned and said, "I just thought of what some people would say, if they saw us, saw us being friends. Stupid idea—sorry, I just remembered some of the names I've been called."

"You mean from people like Rutherford Grimes, the last. I'd say the third, but I hope he's the last of his line. He and his friends are a—holes, end of story. Come on, don't let memories destroy the magic."

"Your right." Winter exclaimed, as the two embraced again.

Winter asked, "Before we go, I've got to know, why does Sybil like squash?"

"Well it's like this. When this dock was conceived, Father and the twins would work down here and Betty would gather squash from the nearby garden. They'd place the basket on the built part of the dock and then go into the cove summerhouse for lunch. They started to notice that some of the squash were missing. Well, to make a long story short, Father decided to put squash down on the deck and wait in hiding to see what happened. Sure enough, that's how he figured out what Sybil was up to. He soon turned on the old Monsterjunkie magic and started feeding her himself. Consequently, the rest of us learned, through his patience, how to feed her, as well. As you come to know her, you will notice she has her own issues, she searches for an equally majestic partner to no avail and, we think, it saddens her."

"Amazing, simply amazing," Winter whispered, as she stared at the starry sky.

The two linked arms and walked back to the Manor.

∞ 15 ∞

'Thunder'

During their return through the garden of exotic plant species, Winter was curious about Thunder, the pigmy elephant.

Winter inquisitively commented, "Thunder is such a beautiful creature, reminding one of a baby elephant. Yet she, she is a she, right, is actually a pigmy elephant, totally indicative of your father's ability to collect mysterious pets.

Indigo smiled at her awareness, "Thunder is a precious treasure my father rescued from a circus with the specific idea of making money from her. He also saved her mother, Serenity, at the same time. She is currently at a sanctuary called Heart Haven, located in the Great Crater, in a safe, somewhat hidden, location in Madagascar."

She does communicate. By stomping her feet, her mother knew it was her and understood. She'd talk back, which Thunder understood. It was amazing. Actually I have a poem on my phone about Thunder and Serenity. Would you like to hear it?"

"You're kidding? You're not. Yes."

They paused and Indigo called up the poem...

Thunder, Thunder fills us with fear, awe and wonder
This crushing noise asks, "What can I ruin or plunder?"

In this story, no storm or gale, just the thumping of feet,
Pounding legs tell a tale with a great rhythmic beat.

The stomping of a young elephant—faithful and true,
pounds a message to her mother—captured and blue.
This powerful sound alerts, and thrills all of her clan.
Her feelings, hope and strength ring through the land.

On the great open plain, Thunder stomps her way south
her pounding communicates true—no need for a mouth.
On the same great plain, Serenity connects to her sound.
They come closer and closer—their joy is unbound.

"What a meaningful message. Who wrote that poem?"

Shyly, Indigo confessed, "A few months ago my brother, Crow, and I joined to sketch it, this is just a part of it. You can never meet him, but my Grandfather Ernest was a poet, he would have loved this, because it's about a special part of our family."

"From the poem, it's obvious you both love Thunder like a faithful pet, this day has been an incredible whirlwind.

Indigo had one more point to share, "You'll never believe it but Thunder totally jams on music, she loves the piano in particular."

Winter smirked, "OK , you know I'm an artist, but you don't know, I loovvveeee to play the piano."

"No way, how good are you? You can serenade Thunder tomorrow morning, I'd love to hear you play, too."

"So many unbelievable introductions, too many things to think of, I'm sacked, let's go back now," Winter said.

❧ 16 ❧

The Monster Ball

Sunday morning, Winter sat with Frances and Betty by their cottage, as she sketched the two in front of their flower garden. When she finished, she embraced both of them and said good-bye. After she returned to her room, she packed her bags and Indigo, along with Thunder, accompanied her to the library where the Steinway grand piano was acoustically positioned. Winter looked at Thunder, "Is there any song you particularly enjoy? OK, maybe you'll enjoy the following jazzed-up versions of Debussey's, 'Claire de Lune,' and based on the poem, the Grateful Dead's 'Bird Song.'

Throughout both songs Thunder seemed to smile, perhaps in appreciation or simply because she loved piano music, but to the jazz beat she wagged her tail, almost. Finally, Winter slid off the bench onto her knees and she enjoyed a gentle, loving hug with Thunder, who caressed her back with her trunk.

Joined by Pandora, after she discretely listened to the music, they casually walked to the foyer. Mentioning the wonders she was shown and the joy it brought to her, she thanked Pandora for the opportunity to visit their world.

"Thank you sooo much for allowing me to visit your manor, I have learned so much. Frances and Betty, and Beauregard... Please thank Dr. Monsterjunkie, he is a remarkable man, sorry I couldn't thank him myself. And I realize Crow is with Beau at his cottage or with his pets, let him know I enjoyed meeting him, too."

Winter, with her bags in hand, and Indigo walked to the front gate to wait for her father who was scheduled to pick her up soon.

Indigo commented, "I'm glad you enjoyed this experience, I know I did. I'd like us to plan for some things down the road, I think M J Manor needs more people to support the effort. I think we should bring in some friends including Crow's buddies if they're open minded, like you."

Suddenly Winter's face lit up, "I've got an idea. Why don't we do a 'Monster Ball,' a party to celebrate our friendship and the incredible nature of Monsterjunkie Manor? Just like you said, we'd only have people we trust that can handle something like this. Since they're not really monsters, we could put a question mark in back of Monsters or something clever like that. I'd love to illustrate the written invites, what do you think? You know, the more I think about it, how monsters look, supposedly strange or threatening, the more I realize that they're really not monsters, the monsters are the people who wear masks of respectability and goodness, but inside are actually vicious and cruel, like Rutherford J Grimes III."

"You're so right. That's it exactly. And yes, the Monster Ball is a great idea.

Let's start planning tomorrow. I'll get my parents on board and we'll see about interesting people we can invite."

Winter saw her father's car approach, they hugged each other quickly as he pulled up. She got in and Indigo waved to them, as they pulled away. She watched the car roll into the distance. As she returned to M J Manor, she did so with an entirely new feeling about her home, a gratifying sense of pride.

∞ 17 ∞

To the Principal's Office

O n Monday morning, Ed Hodges sat uncomfortably in Principal Sally Connors' office, waiting for his 9:00 am appointment. He was never a big fan of going to the principal's office, for whatever reason. Nevertheless he did want to get to the bottom of the incident that occurred with his son Mark last week.

Sally, wearing a well-tailored grey pinstripe business suit hurriedly entered and, as she became comfortable, she said, "Sorry I'm late, but I've been running behind all morning and I sort of know why you're here. Please give me the details of what happened, based on what Mark shared."

"Apparently Rutherford Grimes, 'Ruth' as his friends call him, decided to gang up on Mark with several of his buddies. They roughed him up and gave him a bloody nose. That's disturbing, but what really bothers me is their reason for doing this, which was an indirect attack on Mark's sister, Winter. They used scurrilous names directed at her in Mark's presence last week and, apparently, on other occasions, too. Those comments are completely unwarranted and vicious, and I'd like to know what you'll do to end this abuse."

Principal Sally Connors leaned forward, looking directly at Ed, "We have a 'no tolerance policy' about bullying here and I can assure you, Mr. Hodges, that we'll do everything in our power to see that

Mark and Winter are not abused again by Rutherford Grimes and his friends or by anyone else.

I received a call from Ruth's father late Friday afternoon after the conference we attended. He claimed Mark provoked the fight and he has witnesses to prove it. I know the boys and I have already talked to all three. They've stuck to Ruth's story. I gather also that the incident occurred off school property in Foggy Point Park. That limits my jurisdiction for now, but it is clear to me what I need to do on campus."

Ed asked, "Do you believe their story, Ms. Conners? You heard my speech on bullying at the PTA meeting and you know how the bullying game is played. They are using the very tactics I described, including taunting, secret backstabbing and provoking victims when the moment's right. It's all part of the game and that is exactly what's happening here."

"I'm aware of that, but to be effective, we need to coordinate our people on campus to monitor this situation and then take action. Believe me, Ruth has been schooled in the fine art of evasiveness, knowing his legal rights and, most importantly, how to control people around him—skills which he has, undoubtedly, learned from lack of parenting. His father works and plays all the time and his mom is busy doing one thing or another.

I won't say anything more about that, but here's what I'll do. I'll brief both of my vice principals, Mr. Cisneros and Mrs. Clark, Mark and Winter's teachers, and, if they witness any bullying, we'll take punitive action against anyone who does it. Believe me, I don't want anybody to live in fear—not on my turf, so I'll be more observant also, this should correct the problem, OK?"

"Thanks, Ms. Conners. I don't want my kids to relive what happened to them in the last school they attended. And I think you're in a much better position to control it in a school this size."

"It's good you have kids who speak their minds. The most damaged victims of these sorts of things are the quiet ones who are too embarrassed or afraid to talk. They're the ones who have breakdowns or, tragically, take their own lives."

They continued discussing several other school issues. Finally, Ed left Sally Conners' office only somewhat reassured, still concerned about his children.

❦ 18 ❦

Schnoggin Knockers Unite

In another area of the school, Crow was working diligently to complete one part of a timed standardized test. A solid student, he felt confident about his performance and he didn't let his recent connection to class members distract him from the task at hand. When Edgar saw him before class and gave him a fist bump of "Thanks," he suspected that things were cool with the guys. During one of the breaks during the morning, Crow briefly teased them with the idea of visiting M J Manor. They were excited and wanted in. The four agreed to meet in the park after school.

They converged at a private place in the park to discuss their options and make some tentative plans.

Edgar spoke first to Crow, "I got'ta tell you, I've been thinking about your place nonstop. There were no other options, so I had a lot of time this weekend. When you stepped in front of that hysterical ape, you convinced me you had steel cajones."

Crow laughed, "I don't know about steel cajones, but good schnoggins."

The group exclaimed, "Schnoggins?" then started laughing at the word.

Todd asked, "What the heck's a schnoggin'?"

"It's a word I learned from my father who picked it up from his father. Great Grandfather was a German emigrant from Bavaria to

America. He had his own funny vocabulary, his word for balls was schnoggins. My Grandfather Ernest passed the word to my father when they used to capture some pretty strange animals together and, sometimes when the tension was great, an amusing comment about schnoggins would lighten the moment."

Larry interrupted him, "You got that right."

"This one rare monkey grabbed Great Grandfather by the schnoggins and Conrad decked him, shouting, 'Leave my schnoggins alone.' The way my father told it, it was so funny my sides hurt from laughing. Apparently, Conrad used to say his 'schnoggins knocked,' whenever he got close to finding some really special animals."

Todd shouted, "Hey that's it, we're the 'Schnoggin' Knockers.' That's got'ta be our name from now on. What do you think?"

Larry shouted, "Yea, the Schnoggin' Knockers kick a–."

∞ 19 ∞

The Grimes' Gang

O n the other side of the same park, Winter took advantage of the extra time and decided to create some sketch work by the park lake, the community's version of Walden Pond. She left a text message for Indigo, asking if she'd like to join her in the park. She saw several overreaching trees near the water and began sketching them, the birds on their branches and in the water. Thinking about last weekend and sketching, placed her in a relaxed and reflective mood.

A little over a hundred yards from her location in a stand of trees, Rutherford J. Grimes III sat with his two "closest" companions, Nick and Logan, who, depending on the occasion could be: sidekicks, cronies, bodyguards, stooges, flatterers, clowns, or unabashed a–kissers. They had just joined him. The Grimes kid passed them two Havana cigars, which his father had illegally brought to the US and all three of them lit up puffing away—each imagining himself to be a future executive, enjoying a privileged luxury—real 'masters of the universe.'

Nick exclaimed, "Wow, I can see why your old man smuggles these into the country."

Logan asked, "Ruth, how does he get them in."

"One of his employees regularly picks them up in Canada. If you think that's good, wait till to you try this," as he pulled out a flask he had concealed in his backpack. "This is from a bottle of cognac that I requisitioned from my father's liquor cabinet. It's premium XO stuff. He has so many, he won't even know it's missing." He passed it around to the approval of each.

Ruth interrupted their fantasy, "Good job with the principal. With my father's phone call and your stories, we've heard the last from that wimp and his pathetic family.

"I wish they'd create a state and put all the fags, illegals, welfare parasites and other retards in one place. I'm sick of this country being overrun with so many weaklings."

Nick chimed in, "You got that right, I heard in some states they'll be in the majority in about 10 years or so."

Logan, reinforcing him, said, "Can you imagine, people like us being in the minority? That totally sucks."

Ruth endorsed their chorus of hate, as he stood and delivered one of his words- from-dad harangues, "Dad has joined a new group that's lobbying to really tighten up penalties against illegals and make immigration to our country a lot tougher. When I get some literature on it I want you to pass it along to your parents and friends. Dad said, if we don't stop this now, it'll be too late before we know it."

They affirmed their agreement in a chorus of expletives leveled against all of the groups Ruth named. As Ruth walked around Nick and Logan, he caught a glimpse of someone from the corner of his eye. "Hold on a minute guys, I think I just spotted an example of what we were just talking about. Come here and take a look."

The Schnoggin' Knockers were huddled around Crow, who was temporarily assuming a leadership position. He said, "Listen guys, I'm going to try to talk my father into letting you spend the weekend just like he did for one of Indigo's friends. That way you'll see what our place is really all about."

Larry spoke up, "Awesome man, I can't wait."

Todd started laughing and said, "I just remembered something my sister told me. She's a sophomore at Maine College. She said her Roman history teacher said that when Romans took an oath they held their schnoggins. They believed that if you broke the oath you risked becoming sterile or worse, I guess they took it pretty seriously. Maybe that's what we have to do with what we see there, because based on what we saw, it's pretty out-there stuff. Crow, what do you think?"

"Todd, you remember the strangest things, but we need do something like that to protect my family and the estate, even if it means taking an oath. That's what we'll decide when I get my father's green light on this. Let's take the oath now."

The four each raised a fist into the air, shouting, "Schnoggin' Knockers. Schnoggin' Knockers. Schnoggin' Knockers." Todd interrupted their chorus when he saw Winter running in their direction, clutching her ISketch to her chest. "Hold on guys, isn't that Winter Hodges. It looks like she's really upset. What is it with this park and the Hodges family?"

The four sprinted in her direction and, as they intercepted her, Crow asked, "What's wrong, Winter? What happened?"

She fell to the ground and began sobbing. She finally composed herself and spoke, "I unexpectedly ran into Ruth Grimes and his two cronies, Logan and Nick."

Todd went to her and grabbed her arm, helping her up and said, "Tell us everything that happened. You're among friends now. We'll help you, OK?"

She held on to Todd and said, "I was sketching down at the lake. It was great for a while, but those three snuck up on me and Ruth grabbed my pad, while the other two began calling me names. I'm not going to repeat them, they're too hateful, you know what they are. They started looking at my sketches and ridiculing them. They began tossing the pad around to each other, playing keep away."

She paused, looking at Crow and sobbing, "They asked if Betty and Frances were my sisters. They said they looked like me. I'm so sorry Crow, I took out all of the other sketches of the manor I made, except for that one, because I love those two so much. I told your mom and Indy that I'd be careful and now I've blown it."

Crow immediately intervened, "Winter, it's OK. That's not going to hurt my family. You haven't blown anything, alright?"

Larry asked, "Did they touch you or physically hurt you?"

"When I intercepted my sketchpad, I bumped into Nick and he grabbed my behind. When I got my pad and started running, Logan tripped me and I fell and they laughed at me. They reeked of tobacco and booze, I think they were drunk. When I started to run this way, they took off in the other direction."

Todd said, "These scumbags assaulted you. They should face charges and we need to decide what to do next."

Crow said, "I'm going to call Indy to get her down here as soon as possible, I'll be right back."

When Crow left, Winter said, "I know I screwed up keeping that sketch where other people could see it. I'd tell you what it was, but I promised..."

Edgar interrupted her and said in a soothing voice, "Listen girl, I know you're upset, but now you need to chill. Crow gave you the straight stuff when he said he was cool with what happened. Crow went to bat for me in a nasty situation and I trust him completely now."

Crow returned and said to Winter, "She'll be here shortly, I told her everything, and she specifically said not to worry about the sketch, OK?"

"Thanks, Crow."

Larry asked, "Is there anything else you can remember they did?"

Winter answered, "No, not really, but something just struck me. I think Grimes played his two buddies to do most of this, I saw him standing back and smiling at their stupid antics."

Todd said, "That's it; that's the way he always operates. If this goes to the police, trust me, his old man will find a way to save his sorry butt."

The five remained silent, until Crow recognized his sister pulling into the school parking lot across the street in a small manor maintenance four-wheel drive buggy. Indigo had her license and drove occasionally, but mostly on the estate. She knew Winter was terribly upset and needed her help. She quickly came to the group and went immediately to Winter and hugged her.

She said, addressing all of them, "Here's what I think we should do. I'll drive Winter home and stay with her while she explains this to her father. I'll recommend that we go to the police to file a formal complaint but, before doing that, I'd like her to talk to our family attorney. My mother is talking to him, as we speak. Winter, let's go to your house and I'll get in touch with my mom there."

Turning to the boys, she said, "I think the best thing you can do is to go back to school and see if you can find the principal or one of her assistants to explain what happened. I think the sooner we tell somebody the better, if they've gone home already, find any teacher that's available, OK?"

Edgar, Larry, and Todd, captivated by her beauty and her take-control attitude, simply nodded in agreement.

Todd broke the trance, advanced to Indigo and extended his hand to her. As she accepted his hand, he took a formal bow and kissed it saying, "Mademoiselle Monsterjunkie, it's an honor to make your acquaintance, even under circumstances as inauspicious as these."

This broke his fellow Schnoggin' Knockers out of their temporary stupor into a quizzical smiles, as Indigo, very pleased, replied, "What an elegant gesture. I too am honored, gallant knight, protector of friend and family, and I now embrace you as a friend." She walked over to him and gave him a hug.

"I am beyond words, fair, fair Indigo," he said trying to sound Shakespearean, while struggling to compose himself with the unexpected intimacy.

Larry, Edgar, and Crow could barely keep from laughing out loud. Todd was the epitome of cool, he thought. Even Winter broke into a smile.

∝⧜

The four of them watched Winter and Indigo walk to the car and, when they were out of earshot, Edgar, Larry, and Crow burst into laughter. Larry went over to Todd and got him into a friendly headlock and said, mocking him, "Is Monsieur Toddy captured by Mademoiselle M J?" They all chortled as Larry continued, "It's noogie time," as he lightly knocked his head with his knuckles and then let him loose from his headlock.

When they stopped teasing him, Larry asked Todd, "Where did you pick up that formal lingo?"

"I spent some time in Europe with my family. You just kinda get used to it." Then after a pause he said, "Crow, I think I'm in love with your sister. She is seriously gorgeous and probably brilliant. I can still smell her scent on my shirt. I won't throw this one in the wash soon, maybe never. I think we were all blown away by the way she handled this."

Crow smiled and said, "My grandfather, Ernest, perhaps was not as formal as my great grandfather; however, I remember he spoke in such an elegant way. Anyway, she's good at it, she knows how to handle my parents, especially my mother. I think we have a new ally now."

"Speaking of gorgeous, your mom is like knock-your-socks-off beautiful. What happened to you, Crow?" asked Larry. They laughed.

"I'm not so bad. I've got it where it really counts."

"Where's that, man?" asked Edgar.

"In the schnoggins, where else?" Everyone laughed.

They walked to school, but found no one there. They saw only two janitors sweeping the gymnasium and one emptying trash. They decided to wait until tomorrow to tell anyone.

Pandora's attorney briefed Ed and Winter, and Indigo joined them when they went to the police station. Indigo noticed a difference in the desk officer. When Ed informed her of who the complaint was against, it seemed to make her a bit uneasy. They filed the complaint and left shortly after the desk officer questioned them on some of the particulars of the paperwork. Ed said he'd inform Sally Connor of what happened.

Ed gave permission for Indigo to spend the night with Winter at their home. Indigo and Winter intended to figure out a plan for the Monster Ball. She went home briefly to get Pandora's permission and get an overnight bag. Then she returned to Winter's place.

❧ 20 ❧

Having a 'Ball'

After a late-nighter, when Winter and Indigo talked about the day's events, they finally concluded what they must do for the 'Ball.' They agreed each one of them would invite a person they could trust. With the inclusion of Crow and his three friends, that would bring the list to eight; the first youthful group to attend such an introduction. If that worked, they could bring more people for a similar event, later.

They went to school together the next day and discovered that Logan and Nick had called in sick. However, Ruth was at school and, as he passed Crow in the hallway, he said, "Good Morning, *Crom-well.*" He sneeringly emphasized 'Crom.' Crow did not reply. Before he caught up with his sister and Winter, he had an idea.

"Indy, Winter, let me check your purses; I need to get something. I know that sounds weird, but I promise I won't do anything wrong. Trust me."

The two girls stared at each other in confusion, as he asked again.

Indigo said, "What are you up to?"

"Come on, you'll see. Turn your heads. I don't want you to look." He quickly opened both, found what he wanted immediately, returned their purses and dashed off.

Later in the day at lunch, the Schnoggin' Knockers met near the edge of the athletic field. Recapping their experiences yesterday, they

107

thoroughly beat the topic to death, but they also expressed the hope Crow and Indigo would set up the Monster Ball at M J Manor. As they talked, Crow noticed that Ruth walked onto the field with three girls. Crow could see by his gestures he was bragging about something to them.

He said, "Check out who just came onto the stage, did you notice that Logan and Nick aren't with him? I'll be right back," as he dashed towards Ruth and his group before the Schnoggin' Knockers could ask what he was doing or object to it.

Ruth was surprised to see him brazenly break into the group. Crow spoke directly to him saying, "Hi, you greeted me in the hallway this morning, but we've never met, the name is Ruth, right?" Crow pronounced it, as the Biblical Ruth and then said, "Or is it Ruthy?" Before Ruth could respond, he exclaimed, "I did what you asked, I found a tampon for you," as he quickly stuffed one into Ruthy's shirt pocket. Ruth pulled away from Crow's surprise action.

He then turned to the girls in mock seriousness saying, "Ruthy's had an unusually heavy flow this morning." Before Ruth could speak because, at this point, he was nearly apoplectic, Crow continued, "Help me out here, Ruthy. A couple days ago, I heard Logan and Nick say that the closest you'd ever get to a girl would be the tampon you gave her, is that true? Or, actually, is that your goal in life—being a tampon?"

Ruth, enraged and trying to say something coherent could only squeak out, "Who'd you think you are? Who'd you think you are?" as he ran after Crow, who dashed back to the Schnoggin' Knockers. Ruth was gaining on Crow when Crow ducked and veered left; as a result Ruth fell, rolling in the grass. He got up and continued his chase, but he came to a halt when Edgar came between them.

Getting into Ruth's face, Edgar said, "You got a problem with my brother here?"

Ruth, seeing he was completely surrounded, began to back away.

Todd taunted him, "Ruth, you look a little pale. Are you having trouble finding someone to abuse."

Crow interrupted, "Let me help you on the pronunciation; its Ruth or Ruthy. He had a problem, which I tried to help him with. "You see," as he walked over and pulled the tampon from his shirt pocket, "What do you call it when somebody has both male and female stuff? Help me out here Todd, you're the word-meister. Brandishing the tampon, Crow said, "Ruthy is having an extra tampon day."

"I think the word is hematology or something like that," Larry suggested.

"That's funny, the word is hermaphrodite," Todd stated.

"Wow, what a tragedy. We won't tell, Ruthy. We know what an upstanding guy—or is it girl?—you are," Larry chimed in, sarcastically.

They silently moved in around Ruth, forming a close circle. They said nothing more. Their cold stares told the story. Ruthy kept turning around looking for a place to go. He was suddenly seized with nausea and bent over. The four backed off when he started to vomit. Todd gestured they ought to leave.

Mid-week, Crow asked his buddies if they wanted to come to explore the estate over the weekend? They were amazed, a rather quick invitation and only Larry said he might have something planned already, but would check.

The next day they, Larry included, agreed to meet Crow Saturday morning to hang out and take a tour of the monster mansion digs.

⊗ 21 ⊗

The Gathering

Saturday morning, Todd's dad, Winston, gave the Crew a lift to the mansion.

"Thanks for the ride, Dad, Crow texted he'd be out in a second, we're going to have a trippin' weekend. Larry's dad'll pick us up, luv ya" He gave his dad a partial hug.

Crow in cosmic trunks, met his friends saying, "Hey, brought your suits, right? Let's take your stuff upstairs. You can change into your suits later, maybe we'll go snorkeling in the cove."

"Let's start the morning with a tour of the underground base-ment complex, where there's an aquarium, sanctuary and laboratory designed for land animals and aquatics," suggested Crow. He described the crypto-lab as they walked through the underground passage, "The crypto-lab is encased in a glass bubble in the center of the main aquarium, accessed by an underground passageway including several ventilation and power shafts and are secured by two 'coded' doors. The lab is filled with frozen tissues, eggs, embry-os, sperm and DNA samples of endangered and extinct species, dedicated to medical and genetic rebuilding, which consumes the majority of Dad's time.

"During the initial planning, Great Grandfather Conrad, insisted on this design. It was way ahead of its time. The circular complex is a transparent hub, the thick laboratory spoke-like rooms are attached, providing complete visual contact to the exterior portion of this aquatic wheel.

"The other two circle complexes have island-like centers accessed by underground passages and overhead bridges, as well. Also, there are two more snake-like aquariums, meandering among the other complexes and an aviary, accommodating multiple bird populations. One of the aquariums has a flow-through system, simulating a river or stream. Water is pumped in from Cryptic Bay.

"Two new complexes are under construction, along with several new holding areas. The complete complex includes a south side administration office with passageways to different observation points. At the east end of the complex is a substantial maintenance garage with an alternate roadway leading to Foggy Point and points beyond."

Crow explained, "As a child, I was totally wigged out by this 'save the world' zoo. The animals were scary, I thought they would have me for dinner. And the metal beams with circular holes were way too weird. Finally, I have come to appreciate the vision required to dream beyond, to make it happen. I guess I'm part of all of this," as he waved his hand. "It's unlimited what people can do if they are determined to save something precious."

"Look at these turtles, aren't they magnificent? They were techni-cally extinct, until my father spoke to a Buddhist monastery and several private collectors, they are allowing us to use our tools to bring these amazing turtles back. My father would have to explain the meticulously crafted details of the *in vitro* breeding program. Actually, in cooperation with Asian and American visionaries working in harmony, all this was possible." They all stood in complete bewilderment in front of the massive tank. Crow looked to his right and saw Aaron, the grad student, approach underwater with several of the amazing turtles.

"We're in luck, this is Aaron, our grad student swimming with the Yangtze soft shells." Aaron, making bubbles with his diving equipment, waved to the group. "He works here regularly and, eventually, he will be a member of the family in this facility when we find the funding necessary for the new expansion."

"How'd you find and manage to get, what did you call them, Yangtze turtles? Especially among collectors—you know, they're a stingy bunch who don't give up their precious treasures easily," Edgar said. "My dad collects stamps and he won't give them or sell them to anyone. He won't even let me touch'em."

"Good question; the Buddhists we spoke to were thought to have one turtle in a lake in Viet Nam, when they finally agreed to share, much to our surprise, there were several, some of them youthful and in surprisingly good condition. There followed a worldwide campaign, especially in Asia, to acquire others for breeding. We dogged the task and were able to work with several anonymous collectors to establish our program. I'm too young to remember any of this, but we have a solid chance for a rebirth of this rare group of turtles."

"Will they ever be able to return to a natural river and have a presence again?" asked Todd.

"Don't know, that's why we're doing this. The people who lived with them for generations also want to reintroduce them. We're getting there, but you know we have to be careful, otherwise all this effort is a bust. In a few years, based on environmental changes, they'll get to hang out in the wild again. They're like the Vietnamese turtle Hoan Kiem, but way more difficult to find."

"Come on, I want to show you some other rare gems. Look at these Baijis, Chinese river dolphins. In nature, they are called 'Goddesses of the Yangtze,' what a cool name."

"Are all your animals from China?" Larry wondered.

"Until a few years ago, China was going down the drain, the animals in China were disappearing overnight, the environment was totally high risk. Apparently, for no reason, they got it, so did many others around the world, perhaps you saw the BBC interview with Dr. Lin Wong, severely criticizing the dangerous conditions. Recent progress has given worldwide ecologists a ray of hope. His more recent comments were a dramatic turn around from his initial hopeless comments."

The group continued around the circle of this aquarium and transitioned into the adjacent lab areas. Crow paused briefly and remarked, "The lab we just passed is one of the primary research groups dealing with the feline immunodeficiency disease epidemic. Next, I'll show you a cat we're trying to sustain, trying to create a cure, giving us all kinds of data on immunity. We hope this will end this epidemic."

"Here is the Scottish wildcat colony, they have a Scottish Highland simulation to hang out in."

They moved to the front of the environment and, in the distance, everyone could see a Scottish wildcat languidly draped over the lower branch of an oak tree. Two kittens cavorted nearby.

Crow began, "The Scottish wildcats are endangered and it is in danger of loosing its distinctive character by interbreeding with similar lines—domestic house cats, for instance. Our cats are carefully bred from wildcats selectively taken from Great Britain and European sanctuaries. Besides being a wonderfully independent breed, these guys are providing us with genomic information we think can help us solve the feline immunodeficiency disease problem. We know, for sure, not a single wildcat has contracted the disease."

"Now, guess what? I'm going to show you several special simulated habitats currently holding a number of endangered mammals, you're gonna love 'em."

In all ways possible these environments, the aquatic habitats, replicated the specific areas on the planet from which the animals were obtained. They arrived first at the red wolf habitat that duplicated an American southeastern eco-system with appropriate flora and higher humidity.

Crow spoke to the group, "The red wolf story is comparable to other predators who are carefully reintroduced into habitats shared by people. Red wolves have been endangered for a long time, with reintroduction efforts going back into the 80's. We've agreed to continue this effort with several groups in the eastern United States.

As one came into view, "Like its grey wolf cousin, the red was thought to be a danger to livestock. Actually the red wolf is almost invisible, often secretive, and sure isn't going to attack large livestock. They hunt small mammals and, on rare occasions, bring down small deer. We're keeping them secure here and, periodically, introduce them to selected sanctuary habitats. Unfortunately, they can breed with coyotes, which means this type of breeding in the wild lessons their chance to remain pure."

As Crow observed another pair furtively staring at the group, he commented, "Also, note this area contains plants equally endangered. But they are not threatened by our red friends. The reds are kind of like the Honshu wolf, who is extinct, but we want them to continue to be viable.

"Let's take a break, then we'll go to the Aviary," concluded Crow.

22

The Aviary

C row led the group to the aviary tucked away between two of the large aquariums. They entered through a double door and crossed an interior marshland, where a flock of Yuma clapper rails did a synchronized turn. The rails were a mottled tanish-brown, not as squat as a duck and had elongated beaks, but the sound of their wings was singular.

"They get to be here because the riparian and marshland areas throughout the world are failing. Recent restoration projects in this state and in California have helped but they really need help from people like us. In the next section I'll show you the results of our work," Crow commented. Crow was energized and the rest of the crew tried to stay up with him.

They moved through another set of double doors to the next habitat, which was set up for least terns, migratory birds, brought here for breeding and recovery so they can return to their migratory patterns. The terns were classic in terms of profile, the top of the head was black reaching down to a straight, pointed orange beak with a white mask, otherwise they had grey wings and body with a few darker tail feathers, white everywhere else.

Several workmen stood on top of the structure. The group, looking up, wondered what was going on. With pride, Crow elaborated, "This group of terns is about to be released, hopefully they will rejoin their brothers and sisters and become part of the family—something even a confined sanctuary like M J Manor, never forgets. We also never forget our mission to restore healthy, living friends to active playfulness in the world. Today, these birds are being released to rejoin their air-born brethren in their natural flight patterns. Watch for a minute and they'll open the hatches."

As if they'd received a signal from Crow, the workers opened several large hatches in the glass ceiling. When the canopy was removed, several terns instinctively headed for freedom and, collectively, as if consciousness suddenly overwhelmed them, a wave of hundreds flew to freedom.

Crow continued, "They'll be a healthy addition and will strengthen the tern population."

The next colony was the golden cheeked warblers. A small bird, perhaps smaller than the red-winged blackbird, the warbler had a yellow head with two thin black stripes from a pointed black beak to the rear of the neck, a wider black stripe over the top of the head and was, overall, primarily black with white stripes created by feather ends on the upper wings with a white underbelly.

He explained the experimental nature of the habitat. "The endangered warblers are only found in central Texas and they're not doing well. They only breed in trees of the area, the oak and the juniper ash, I believe. We are attempting to introduce them to other types of trees indigenous to the southwest, hoping they'll have other options. We're cooperating with several groups in Texas and regional sanctuaries, but we don't know if it'll work yet.

"Let's have a look at our neatest project in recent years. My father has been reading about the ivory billed woodpecker for like ten years." They wandered over to the specially controlled environment, a large swamp-like enclosure. He scanned the habitat to locate the focus of his comments and, barely visible, he was rewarded by seeing a woodpecker near the back of the swamp. A larger than normal bird, primarily black with an extended neck and long ivory beak, the ivory billed woodpecker had white stripes from the beak on the sides to the white rear of the wings. The underbelly was black with the underside of the wings being white and black. The most distinctive feature was the plumage-covered, pointed head.

Crow began to describe this bird, "Long thought to be a Lazarus species, two groups were discovered. Our colony, in collaboration with others, will keep these woodpeckers going well into the future. Really, we are one of three lab-sanctuaries in the US who is allowed to hold and breed these birds, the other two are in the southeast. Like its cousin, the imperial woodpecker of Mexico, these birds are among the largest of their species—clearly, among the most beautiful of birds. This bird's wingspan is over thirty inches."

"Now, let me introduce you to Orion, our spix macaw. This one is aptly named for his 'mind' and keen 'insight'. He's a source of hope for all the specimens in our sanctuary."

The macaw nodded to him and gently nuzzled his arm, "Everyone thought he and a few others were the end of the line—until recently several were spotted in their home jungle. He, like many of the endangered, is a victim of black market poachers, along, once again, with massive encroachment on his habitat. Confiscated from a Brazilian dealer, getting ready to sell him to a European buyer, is how we came by him.

"We acquired him many years ago with the idea of letting him finish out his days and then we learned of the discovery of wild spix, unbelievably surprised, we immediately set up a breeding program. Along with a few other institutions, these birds are coming back. We have four young offspring, they'll be bred with others in captivity—and eventually we'll let them breed with their wild friends." He continued, "The Brazilian government has set up a well-protected preserve away from any possible poacher encroachment, where they nurture a group of macaw."

Edgar wanted to know, "Do the macaw repeat what we say?"

Crow laughed, "No, they're just macaws."

Todd asked if this was the end of the ark, he was feeling overwhelmed by the flood of animals, he liked them and the architecture was incredible, but he wanted to get to the cove and relax on the sand.

Actually, this was the end of a spectacular tour. As they moved up the escalator, Todd said to Crow, "This has been so cool, I never realized you had so much knowledge, you must know almost as much as your dad. You have an incredible understanding and these animals are like your pets. This might be your future."

"My father learned from his father and my grandfather, they've accomplished a great deal and, surprisingly, I didn't know how much influence this wildlife has had on me. Tell you the truth, it used to scare me, the animals seemed like prehistoric monsters, I thought they would kill me and maybe eat me. But, over the past few years, I've come to know their true beauty and I guess they are my pets."

As the group went to change cloths, Crow thought about what Todd had said about the possibilities of his future and came to the realization of how lucky he was to be a part of this family, a Monsterjunkie.

∞ 23 ∞

Monster Mash

The following Saturday, after a week of suggestions and planning, much of it accomplished with texting on their phones, the girls finally decided on the theme of the Monster Ball. They agreed there would be costuming, mostly masks, but everyone was free to improvise and create anything they wanted.

Winter crafted a special mask for Crow, and she promised she wouldn't tell anyone what it was. She and Indigo would go as Greek goddesses. Winter insisted Indigo dress as Aphrodite and she would attend the Ball as Athena. They found old magazine pictures and glued them onto flexible, single-sheet cardboard, cut them out and attached colorful ties, which transformed them into masks of the goddesses. They were able to somewhat shape the masks to their faces and, with their styled long hair, they became realistic Greek goddesses.

Indigo found a site on Google that described an easy way to create flowing gowns. As Aphrodite, along with braided gold rope over one shoulder, Indigo used flowing white drapes she found at a used clothing store to create a satin flowing gown. She also incorporated the braided rope to form an elegant headband and a three-stranded belt of twisted golden ribbon tied in a bow at the back. Along with a gold Roman appearing bracelet on her right wrist and a golden bracelet on her upper left arm, with her golden flats, she became a true 'Goddess for the Ball.'

Winter opted to find an inexpensive royal blue gown covered with lighter embroidered small flowers to be the basis for her Athena costume. Contrary to Indigo, she complimented her look with silver adornments.

Todd, anticipating Indigo's presence at the party, decided to dress in a toga, maybe as Caesar. Edgar decided to come to the party as Hercules, wearing an old Steve Reeves picture mask from the 50's movie, billowy black pirate pants with a long sash, an open lighter brown vest and a long headband tied around his mask. Also, he decided to wear an eye patch for authenticity and sport a sword. Larry, a passionate sports lover, would arrive as Tom Brady with a full head mask of the quarterback superstar, an oversized jersey with football pants including pads, carrying a football.

The two unknown guests were Candice Smith, a friend of Indigo, whom she had known since middle school days and, recently, played the lead role in a class play about Russia. She would come as Catherine the Great in a velveteen burgundy gown with a long string of white pearls and a manufactured diamond tiara, serving as her crown. Tara Brown was Winter's friend and, like her, was serious about art. She made a dress, a sheath that was pure nature, with lush greenery and flowers that blended perfectly into the body paint she had on her arms and face. No mask on this nature goddess, she painted her arms and face green. Each eye (lid included), would be the center of a flower, whose petals would reach to her forehead and down her cheeks. Multi colored branches and leaves adorned her arms and face.

Indigo, the hostess of the ball, greeted each new arrival. She and Winter had briefed each new guest about Frances and Betty and to expect the unexpected for the evening. All three of the newcomers were excited about the party; besides, it was great fun to dress up in something completely different, weirdly colorful and playful. Pandora and Talon agreed to make an appearance later and promised to be costumed. Beau would appear last and in a special costume, an arrangement Winter helped Crow negotiate.

There was no formal dinner tonight. Betty and Frances set a buffet, where guests could eat when they pleased. Winter was the first guest to arrive, because she promised to help Indigo with the logistics of the party. She brought the things she had prepared for Crow and Beau. Crow gave her a cordial hug and graciously accepted the costumes and left to take Beau's costume to him and to change into his own secret costume.

Edgar was the first to arrive and, as Hercules, cut an impressive figure. Indigo had heard second hand stories and rumors of what happened on the field with Ruth and Crow, and welcomed the chance to talk to a first hand witness. Crow would only speak of it in generalizations.

Indigo greeted him with a beaming smile and hug, then bowed, "Welcome, mighty Hercules. I understand you showed your mighty prowess at a gathering. Please tell me the tale."

Edgar surprisedly answered her. " Oh Aphrodite, didn't Crow tell you what happened?"

"You know how he is; getting him to talk is like getting blood out of a rock."

Edgar, slightly puzzled, said, "I guess he's different with us, but anyway, I got'ta tell you what he did, he like exposed that creep for what he is. He chopped him down like tree in the middle of the road, it was amazing. When we all like surrounded him, he hurled his guts out."

Indigo questioned, "Pardon me, but what's the deal with the tampon?"

Edgar laughed, "That's what started the whole thing. He humiliated him by like giving him a tampon in front of a group of girls surrounding him. It was hilarious."

"Wow, when he's with you guys, he's really a different person. That's a side of him I'd like to see more often."

"Is he here yet?"

"He's taking care of some things that have to be done. He'll like join us later," as the two observed the arrival of Tara and Candice who drove up together. Indigo introduced Catherine the Great and Nature's Way to Edgar and they were soon joined inside by Athena.

Indigo waited for Larry and Todd. Larry was the next to arrive, "Oh my, Tom Brady my favorite QB. How good is your team going to do this year?"

"Thanks, we're going to the Super Bowl."

"Edgar's inside with the girls. Todd hasn't . . . Wait a minute, I think he's here." After a pause to get a better look at him, she said, "Oh my goodness, it's Julius Caesar, right out of our English book." She and Larry started to laugh."

Todd strode toward Indigo. Standing in front of Indigo in his Roman toga, he bowed to her saying, "I am, indeed, honored to stand before the Goddess of Love. Rome worships you.

Indigo laughed, finding it unnecessay to tell him that she was a Greek goddess, not Roman. Instead she said, "Welcome to a household where love is preeminent."

Caesar replied, "I am honored to cross the threshold of your Temple."

Larry thought, *Is he going to worship her right here, or what?*

24

A Special Being

The group went to the buffet table set up in the dining room, removed their masks and began enjoying the food. They were introduced to Betty and Frances, who entertained them with stories about Talon and Pandora and the history of the Monster-junkie house. After awhile, Betty and Frances returned to the kitchen.

Todd whispered to Indigo, "Where's Crow?"

"I think he's cooking up something special, I'm sure he'll be here soon."

Frances returned and announced, "Master Crow wanted you to greet the next guest. He told me to tell you that it would be the only 'true' monster in the house tonight." She walked away and, shortly, a completely cloaked figure entered the room. Everybody grew silent as the figure removed the black hood from his face. The group gasped when they saw the mask of Rutherford J. Grimes III.

Todd smiled and asked, "Do you speak?"

Then in a voice that was a fairly good imitation of Grimes, "Of course I speak, Daddy says it's OK. I'm Ruth to my closest associates or, to some people more recently, "Ruthy."

They shouted their approval and everyone in the room relaxed and pretty much guessed it was Crow, but it was fun continuing the ruse.

Edgar asked, "Is it true that you barfed your guts on the play-ground recently?"

Ruthy answered, "That's true, a group of ruffians attacked me and I thought it was the best way to express myself."

Candice asked, "This is a little awkward, but recently, have you been compared to a woman's hygienic product?"

Ruthy said, "Yes, I have. That's right, it's a tampon, if you must know. It's actually been a life long dream of mine to 'be' a tampon, but regrettably no one has stepped forward to allow my dream to come true."

Tara asked, "Don't you feel some remorse for the way you treated Winter Hodges?"

Ruthy answered, "Daddy has forbidden me to ever use that name. In fact, it has been banned from our household forever."

Indigo asked, "What's your goal in life, other than being a tampon?"

"I'm glad you asked that, because, all my life, I've worn this mask that you see now. I'm prepared at this moment to tear it off and show you who I really am," as he pulled away the mask to reveal Crow's face made up as a vampire.

He said, pointing at his fangs, "My best skill, sucking blood and hope from my victims, is what you see before you, a vampire."

Everybody clapped their approval, the Schnoggin' Knockers went forward and embraced him. The two new girls, Tara and Candice, introduced themselves and congratulated him. Suddenly, the latest rock music began to play and the group paired up and began to rock, while Todd went to talk to Indigo.

In a little while, Frances made an announcement, "May I have your attention, please. Lady Pandora and Master Talon have arrived and wish to meet you."

They entered the room together. Talon wore an elegant formal Mandarin high-collared white Tuxedo, one Conrad actually wore in Europe and, through his father, was willed to Talon. Pandora wore a steelblue/black long dress with a plunging neckline, a steelblue serape cape draped over her shoulders. Pandora's two-tone blue shoes completely matched her simple silver with bluish jade necklace, earrings and bold, diamond-studed dinner ring.

Talon announced, "Good evening ladies and gentlemen, my name is Talon Monsterjunkie and this is my lovely wife, Pandora. We are pleased you could join us this evening. We will converse with you shortly, but before we do, we'd like to introduce you to one more special guest."

As Frances brought in a large antique European carved chair, placing it at the entrance to the dining room, Talon continued, "Beauregard, or Beau as we lovingly call him, is a special being, please notice that I use the word 'being,' you'll see why shortly. Brace yourself for a most unusual experience, but one that should be enlightening. If you like, pull up chairs in front of his, because I know you'll have numerous questions.

When everyone was settled, Talon gestured to the hallway and Beau entered the room. He was dressed as an enormous crow, his head covered by a massive crow's head and a long black cloak that went all the way to the floor. The only accessories were white silk gloves.

He spoke, "First of all, I'd like to thank the Monsterjunkie family for inviting me here this evening. I'm especially pleased to see seated among you, Winter Hodges. Wecome back, Winter."

Winter graciously replied, "Beauregard, I couldn't possibly miss an opportunity to see you again, I love your costume tonight. Even though it is not white, I'm certain Crow loves it, as well."

"It gives me great pleasure to honor him, but it also gives me, what we agreed was best, complete concealment for a time; obviously, we do need to enjoy this occasion and, frankly, to allow people to become used to me."

Todd spoke up quickly, "Sir, if you have some unusual physical characteristic or disability, no one here would think less of you."

"You are a fine young man for being so gracious; however, you'll soon see why that is not the case. Allow me to finish and I suspect most of you will start to discern my identity."

"I was abandoned when I was very young, for what reason I do not know. I was rescued by Master Talon in the wilderness. He saved me, brought me here, educated me, and allowed me to be a part of this family. A thoughtful person might ask, 'Were you a feral child who was abandoned in the wilderness?' My answer would be, no. And, yes, that does create a puzzle, doesn't it? If you weren't a feral child, like Romanus or Remus of Roman lore, who or what are you? The answer, I'm a kind of sentient being and, biologically, I'm a primate."

Looks of comprehension began to grow in the audience and Beau smiled beneath his mask and said, "I see looks that give the answer. Can anyone tell us what they think?"

Candice cautiously spoke first, "Sir, are you, are you what we call a 'Bigfoot'?"

"Indeed, I am."

After initial gasps, the room grew silent for a while until Todd asked, "Sir, would you care to remove you mask?"

"Thank you for asking, young man. As a matter of fact, this outfit is becoming quite warm."

He arose from his chair, removed his head covering, placed it on the floor next to him and did the same for his long cloak. He was dressed in a black tuxedo. He left his white gloves on to complement his evening attire. He presented quite an impressive figure.

The guests were mystified and, as he sat down, Tara posed the next question, "Sir, what do you think of this world, I mean the modern one you live in?"

"Madam, I came from a much simpler existence. This world is obviously more complex and it required me to learn a more complex language than was used among my kind. I don't miss the world in which I was abandoned, though."

Larry asked, "Sir, if you ever go to the outside world, would you try out for the New England Patriots?"

Beau asked Larry, "What position do you think I would play?"

"The whole defensive line," and everyone, including Beau, laughed.

Edgar wanted to ask a question about what they encountered, when they snuck into the Manor, but caught himself, realizing he could expose Crow. However, other questions came fast and furious and, as the evening wore on, Talon and Pandora noticed one of the great joys of effective communication, its bonding effect through understanding and empathy. Everybody got up when Betty and Frances brought in the deserts, which the partiers immediately devoured—Beau included.

Beau instantly became the hit of the evening. Later, Pandora led a tour of the estate house for the girls and Talon did the same for the boys. They all reconvened in the dining room. Crow turned on some music and laughed at one of songs playing, it was the *Monster Mash,* a rock song from the 60s. After awhile, Crow and the rest of the Schnoggin' Knockers broke away from the group and quietly exited the house to a garden nearby. Talon observed them leave and went to a vantage point near a window, where he could observe the four.

The four boys standing in a circle raised their right arms to the sky, fists clenched. With their left hands, they held their crotches. What they were saying was indistinguishable from were Talon stood. He smiled and thought, *I wonder if Todd suggested a Roman oath? What are they taking an oath on, or to whom?* He sensed things were about to change at M J Manor and he secretly harbored a little fear, but mostly hope.

❦ 25 ❦

The 'Masks' Come Off

As the evening concluded, everyone retired to their rooms, the four girls to guest rooms in Indigo's part of the house. She wanted Tara and Candice to get to know each other, so they shared one room, while she and Winter shared the adjacent bedroom. In one guest bedroom next to Crow's, Edgar and Todd bunked, while Larry joined Crow in his room.

Both groups, unbeknownst to each other, agreed they would venture onto the estate grounds for a late night adventure. After shedding their costumes, Crow and Larry met with the other two in their room.

"Let's go to the Bay, maybe just spend some time on the sand," suggested Crow.

Crow continued, "Before we get to the dock, I've got other things I'd like to show you. I didn't even discuss this with my parents, so we need to be quiet and cool, OK?"

They nodded in agreement. Crow put on a small backpack and the four tip-toed down the hallway and out to the garden, where they entered the grounds.

"When we, uh, snuck in the last time, down by the dock, there was something in the water that scared the 'be-jeebers' out of us, if I didn't know better, I'd swear it was a sea serpent," Todd ventured.

Crow calmly answered, "It was a sea serpent. We call her Sybil. In fact, we'll have a good chance of seeing her tonight, since there's a really bright moon. Hey, would you like to feed her, Todd?"

"You're kidding me. No way, feed her?"

"Watch me, I'll show you how it's done. Sybil is way cool and I think mostly vegetarian. If one of us loses a finger or two, we'll know she changed her diet." Larry and Edgar lit up at the prospect and Crow agreed to let them feed her, also.

"I know you probably have more questions for Beau, so first stop is his cottage. We'll talk, let me tell you, he's brilliant and you can ask him anything you like," Crow said.

Todd asked, "How about why he jumped us the first time we were here?"

"That's a good question. He'll give you a straight answer. I don't think he's capable of lying. That crow's head is the only mask he's ever worn. He's studied us carefully, by that I mean humans in general and I think he's kinda' amazed by the things we do. He's a different breed and he doesn't buy into the same BS as humans do—stuff like cruelty for pleasure, dishonesty and bigotry. His insights amaze me at times; he seems to have a window looking into us."

The three arrived at Beau's cottage shortly. Beau greeted them at the front door and they entered his library-living room. The four seated themselves on a very large couch just opposite him. Beau sat in a comfortable easy chair that Master Talon had designed and a local contractor constructed for him, large enough to accommodate his formidable size.

Todd began, "I've got to tell you, Beau, when you jumped out at us. I was as scared as I've ever been. I thought we were goners. I had a vision of our parents trying to identify us at the morgue."

Beau smiled, "I assure you Todd, it was all an act," nodding in the direction of Crow, "Master Crow and I masterminded the encounter for the three of you."

Crow chuckled, as the others shot puzzled glances in his direction, "Hey, don't look at me like that, you were the guys trespassing. We got your attention, didn't we?"

"Damn straight." exclaimed Edgar. "When you stepped in between Beau and us, the first thing I thought was that you must be crazy. Then he obeyed you. Wow, that was unbelievable."

Larry joined in, "I thought you had steel huevos and then you covered our a–s to boot by getting us out of there."

Beau laughed, "I didn't think my performance was that good, but apparently it achieved its purpose. The worst thing that could have happened would have been the three of you laughing at me."

"No way, Josè," Todd exclaimed, "That was Academy Award stuff." After a pause, he said, "You're not a human being, but you're a whale of a lot more human than a lot of the people I know. What do you 'really' think about people?"

Beau pondered, "There's no easy answer to the question, we can talk about basic tendencies, note the 'we', because I consider myself a student of the condition, the 'human' condition. The four of you are obviously true practitioners of your humanity, so this is a 'we' conversation. What startles me is your tendency to cause unnecessary pain to each other. Not 'living' in your world, I only know of it by what I've read and that you are apparently obsessed with war, murder, assault, verbal cruelty and the most terrible and inexplicable of all, the brutal abuse of children by their own parents and relatives."

Beau noticed a subtle change in Larry's demeanor with the last thing he said, and he focused on him, reading his pain. He asked, "Larry, have I touched something that is sensitive to you. In trying to understand this, I hope I haven't caused you to experience the very thing I'm talking about."

Larry became very reflective, as the room became silent. He fought through the painful discomfort and, getting up from the couch, turned to Todd and Edgar, forcing his words, "I know you guys probably wonder why I never talk about my life before I moved to this town with my stepfather and mom. I really didn't think I'd ever talk about it, but being in this place has changed me. I need to tell you."

Composing himself, he continued, "I'm OK with this now, in fact, I need to get it out. My father, well, my father abused me, badly. We won't discuss the details; just use the dark side of your own imaginations and that'll paint pictures of what a deviant person does with his power—in my case, the power of a father over a little boy, his son. He was very clever about concealing all of this and, when my mother tried to take legal action, it was a total mismatch."

"Let's just say, he had masks for his sickness and he could change them as quickly as a slick Vegas card dealer. He used his clever criminal mask to pull off his drug deals and still be friends with cops and judges."

"The courts are mostly clueless about how to deal with abuse, so my mother didn't have a chance. Worst of all was the social worker, she became a tool of my father's, she forced us all to stay together, as a 'family.' Eei, yei, yei, it was a complete farce. We were two people enslaved by a complete bastard."

Larry paused and then continued, "My mother found enough courage to run for her life. She took me and we did the thing: new names, new towns... always changing, always changing. She was hopelessly paranoid he'd find us. I went online regularly to see if I could find out anything about him; then, for some reason I saw an article about a drug dealer who was killed running from the cops. So I guess I looked to see who it was. Sure enough, it was him. I read he burned to death in the wreck, bummer, I couldn't believe it. I might have even laughed."

Larry continued in a more relaxed state of mind, "Finally, finally we were really free and at, almost the same time, my stepfather came into my mom's life. He's an awesome guy—a sports freak, just like me. When my little sister was born, we finally became a real family." His demeanor returned to his usual carefree state and he said, "So, yea, I do know a little something about abuse."

He walked over to Beau and extended his fist to him and Beau, smiling, did the same, as they saluted each other. Larry said, "Thanks Beau, let me tell you, if I could tell you why my dad was like that, I'd do it, but I have no clue. Maybe he came into this world bringing this nasty BS with him, I honestly don't know." He turned to his friends and asked, "What's up? Why the silent game? What the?"

The other three stood up in full support of him, raised their fists to the sky, and shouted, "Schnoggin' Knockers." Beau was somewhat perplexed, but understood.

Candice, Tara, and Winter, followed Indigo into a new holding area, which had just been constructed. The four paused before a small darkened enclosure, where they could see two yellowish cat eyes staring out at them. In silence, with the girls watching, Indigo thrust her hand into the enclosure and grabbed something, which had been indistinguishable in the dark. She gathered it in her arms and embraced it. The three girls were puzzled until she turned and they saw a cuddly, black panther kitten cradled in her arms.

Tara exclaimed, "Oh my goodness, he's so cute." The other two girls joined the chorus of praise. Indigo said it was a male panther.

Winter asked, "What's his name?"

"Inky"

Indigo offered him to the others and they passed him around. Candice was the last one to hold him, she laughed when he began to suck on her finger. Softly she said, "Oh, I'm so sorry Inkydew, you won't get any milk from my pinkydew." As she cuddled and stroked him, she laughed, "Did I just create a rhyme, a pinky for Inky?"

Indigo smiled, pulled a warm bottle from her pack and said, "This is his evening meal, it'll be a lot more what he needs. Let's move on together, we'll take turns feeding him. I have a few surprises left for you."

Tara asked, "Where did your dad get a baby panther? Did he go to Africa recently?"

"This sounds incredible, but he found him in the hills of all places, New Hampshire. There's a lot of so-called panther sightings in North America, but most of them are unverified. We're not even sure what species this little guy is. We're having his DNA checked."

Winter asked, "How did your dad find him?"

"He was roaming around the hills of New Hampshire looking for lizards or something and he heard a gunshot. Of course, all his senses came alive. He figured the sound was several hundred yards away; but, he was totally surprised when, a short time later, he heard a thrashing sound coming through the undercover in his direction.

He saw a wounded black cat coming his way and, immediately, it was obvious it was in trouble. Trailing the cat was Inky, who was barely managing to keep up. It was so sad. The failing mother gave father a look he interpreted as pleading. Her wound was mortal. Actually, father thinks she probably bled to death.

He listened carefully to hear any pursuit and realized no one was following so he found a good place and buried her. When he finished, he saw that this little cutie was disoriented. He gently allowed Inky to comfortably nuzzle in the crook of his arm and brought him back to raise." They all expressed their sadness for the little orphan, as they each held and fed him, Tara even asked if Inky could be her pet panther?

Indigo politely refused saying, "No, sorry, he must stay here. He's still a wild animal and will grow to be over 100 pounds."

Meanwhile, Indigo led them to her evening surprise. She escorted them to Weird Willow, where she had prepared a little campfire site. The four sat down and Indigo lit a fire, while the three girls passed Inky around for petting and feeding. A powerful but invisible flapping occurred overhead, as the three girls stared at the sky, unable to see anything.

Winter asked Indigo, "Is that the enormous bird I got a glimpse of when I was here last time?"

Indigo coyly answered, "Yes, by the way, I have some food in my pack she and a few others around here really love. Would any of you like to feed her?"

"That depends," Tara cautiously replied.

"What is it? asked Candice.

"It's a Pterodactyl. My father brought her back from Indonesia."

"What?" exclaimed Candice. "That's impossible. Those are ancient dinosaur birds, aren't they?"

"Dad decided to verify what a group of people on a small island repeatedly claimed they saw. And beyond belief, they were right, he found a flock of Pterodactyls. He managed, with a lot of clever maneuvering, to get Periwinkle to our estate and now she lives in this tree with several other extraordinary creatures."

"Oh my goodness," exclaimed Candice and Tara.

Winter asked, "How did your father get a hold of Peri, Periwinkle? After all, she is a bird and can fly away?"

Indigo responded "She was injured by something and my father, with the help of villagers, brought her to a safe area where he fixed her broken wing. Then, after a lot of secret arranging and expense, he brought her to the estate."

"Why the name Periwinkle? It's cool and everything, but it just doesn't fit her body. Periwinkle sounds like the name of a kitten or a teddy bear," observed Candice

"Mother named her when she made her first nest for her, she surrounded it with Periwinkle blossoms. Most of the time, we just call her Peri."

Winter wondered, "So, what's the food they like?"

Indigo pulled a bag of marshmallows out of her pack and proudly displayed it to the girls.

Tara said, "You're kidding, marshmallows?"

Indigo discretely replied, "You'll see," as she pulled from her backpack four marshmallow sticks and stuck one on each. She said, "They like their marshmallows roasted instead of cold. Come on, let's light the fire." They each held their sticks close to the fire, careful not to burn them.

Candice's eyes widened, when something nudged her back. Startled, she stared across the fire at Winter and Indigo and nervously asked, "What's pat, patting my back?"

Winter and Indigo began to laugh and, in unison, they said, "Turn around and see."

She hesitantly turned and was immediately face-to-face with a monster, Thunder, a pygmy elephant from Borneo. She exclaimed, "Where? Tell me what a baby elephant is doing here?" She stroked his trunk and asked, "Where's your mama?"

Indigo laughed, "Thunder is a pygmy elephant; that's as big as she gets. And she loves marshmallows. Go ahead she'll take it right out of your hand." Candice, after blowing on it to cool it off, pulled hers off the end of her stick, placed it in her palm and, with no hesitation, Thunder scooped it up with her trunk. Thunder snuggled up close to her, so she could pet her. The other girls put their sticks down and gathered around the pygmy elephant. Tara held Inky and placed the cat close to Thunder, where he could feel her trunk.

Tara said, "This is incredible. We're sitting by a campfire playing with a baby panther and a pygmy elephant, what could possibly top this?"

Indigo gave an interesting response, "To use that old phrase, 'You ain't seen nothin' yet.'"

Beau continued his dialogue with the Schnoggin' Knockers and discussed the mysterious racial/ethnic differences among people—a nearly incomprehensible idea that confounded this articulate and scholarly Bigfoot. He voiced his concerns, "One of the mysteries that is extremely hard to understand is the way humanity divides itself. I understand you are vast in numbers, over the entire world, have different characteristics and, like all other creatures, are territorial, but why does this cause conflict?"

"A lot of it is based on race, Beau; that's the nasty truth of it," Todd answered.

"I know. I've read the same. I don't believe race is a real thing. I think it's a political invention. Many of your scientists think the same. They believe what's called 'race,' is merely the small genetic differences, such as skin color, stature, facial features and hair. Indeed, if you look at a person's genealogy with DNA evidence, it's obvious that an individual is a composite of folks from all over the world—white, black, red, yellow, pink or whatever. What's true is that the DNA of all humans is essentially the same. Even my own is quite close to yours. Master Talon and I have compared our DNA."

Todd supported Beau's observation, "You're right Beau, when people talk about race, they're actually talking about culture combined with physical appearance and, most importantly, years and years of tradition says those things are important."

"I can tell you a few things about this, because my mom is Latina and my dad is African," Edgar added. "Both of those groups were concerned when Mom and Dad got together. Race issues get hot, or even nasty, when people from different groups start to get intimate. It happened to them and it actually ruined some of their friendships. I get those, 'what-is-he-really' looks once in awhile myself. My dad is fairly light skinned and that even causes some groups to make comparisons. I used to be concerned, but I just don't care anymore. I think a lot more people are starting to feel that way."

Crow said to Edgar, "I met your dad only once and the one thing he left me with was the thought of taking the name, Crow, no matter what anybody else said. That was the dig, all I remember from the meeting is that your father is a righteous dude. Everything else about him is just his physical stuff." Edgar and Crow fist bumped in approval.

Beau asked Edgar, "Please, do I understand you correctly, you believe racial and ethnic masks were given to you and yours by society and the real you has nothing to do with any of this non-sense?"

"That pretty well sums it up, Beau."

The girls continued to roast marshmallows, while Thunder strolled off into the bushes. A short time later the four heard a thumping sound. Soon a ground bird casually walked in among them.

"That's a Dodo bird," said Candice, as she stared intently at his advance to the campfire. "Incredible. We studied their extinction in biology. I can't believe what I'm seeing. How did your dad pull this off ?"

Indigo said, "Say hello to Peepers. He is a product of some of the most advanced science around. To answer your question, father became involved with an old friend in Europe who was doing some remarkable things with eggshell DNA and cloning. Peepers is one of their most recent successes. They learned several years ago that eggshells preserve DNA quite well and, then, borrowing genetic material from living animals, filled in the gaps for successful cloning. There are other biologists trying to clone extinct birds, such as the emu of New Zealand and the elephant bird of Madagascar. I'm not sure we could handle those monsters on our grounds. You know, they're really big."

Candice pleaded, "Does your dad teach a biology class I could get into?"

"Yes, at Maine College. I'll talk to him and see if he has any suggestions. Peri should show up pretty soon. She and Peepers are best friends. And talk about the odd couple, I can't imagine two creatures being more different. I have to tell you a funny story. Crow spends a lot of time around here and he got the impression they had been together and thus she is going to lay an egg, it's so bizarre. Dad said it was impossible, but he theorized she could be an amazing rare example of asexual reproduction or it's possible she was fertilized when he brought her here, no one really knows. When she lays an egg and it hatches, it'll be quite an event around here."

Tara and Winter together, whispered, "Wow, amazing."

Shortly, the great beat of wings flapping returned and this time Peri was completely visible gliding to a landing right in front of them. Indigo and Peepers walked forward to greet her. She held in her hand two marshmallows sticks and extended one of them to Peri. The great bird gently plucked it and swallowed it.

Indigo invited someone to feed her the second one. Candice jumped up and cautiously advanced to Peri. The bird did as before and downed the warm white puff, thrilling Candice. She returned to the fire and invited Tara and Winter to feed the great bird. Tara jumped up, with her marshmallow stick. Candice noticed that Winter had tears on her face and she declined to go.

Peri flew back to Weird Willow and Peepers climbed into the little tree house Talon had constructed for him on a lower branch. Winter tried to compose herself, but she was still dealing with an emotional issue.

Indigo finally asked her what was wrong. Winter said, "Believe it or not, I don't really know. I'm happy and sad at the same time, I suppose the puzzlement caught up to me."

Tara said, "Why don't you talk about it?"

"I guess I feel so happy and accepted here, it's really like I'm in some kind of Garden of Eden. This is so beautiful and your friendship is the best I've ever had. I think, I think I secretly wish I could share this with my mom. I still haven't gotten over her death and, strangely, I've thought about her a lot the last few days."

Winter paused for a while before continuing, "I think Crow got it right about the masks, the masks we wear. That's part of my thing too, since there's just the three of us in the family, now. Sometimes I have to put on my mom's mask for Mark, because he needs someone to give him advice or help him with homework, sometimes I need to put on my spouse mask to help my dad out, or cook dinner, or do laundry, or whatever, when he can't handle it.

Then there's the tough bitch mask I put on when I'm dealing with a—s like Rutherford Grimes. I thought I was free of that immaturity when we came here, but it's like a curse that follows us around. Then, there're the other masks people try to put on you, the clever artist's mask, the Bohemian weirdo and, of course, the always popular, dyke mask. I'm none of the above, but I have to live with all of them. Sorry, I apologize for my rant. I'm better now and the last thing I want is to be a 'nosedive.'"

Candice was the first to speak, "Winter, you don't have to apologize to anybody. In the short time I've known you, I already think of you as a friend. If you need help, you can count on me. We'll watch those jerks that hassled you before and I bet the four of us can conjure up some nasty mojo for them, too. Trust me about the masks. Everybody wears them, even my parents, who are good people, still fret over social position. They are nothing like the Grimes' crowd, but they still wear their status masks."

Tara chimed in, "Listen, my mom is a wonderful cook. If you ever get caught up in a situation like that, don't hesitate to call me. We're already friends, so what's the big deal if you and Mark come over for dinner. My mom and dad are a trip, it's like both of their minds have become one, half the time they say things in unison. Anyway, my parents would love to have you and Mark over."

Indigo shared her spirit, "When I first saw you, I knew you would be my friend, and I'm ecstatic we're all friends now. This was a very big get-together for me, since I am finished with my life of privacy behind these walls. My mother understood my dilemma and she and my father took the risk of making our special little world more open. I'm deeply happy we're all here, it means way more to me than you realize."

They continued to talk and tear away masks, as a bright overhead moon illuminated the estate.

The Schnoggin' Knockers bid Beau good night and the four walked in the direction of Cryptic Bay to see if Sybil would make an appearance. They consciously avoided Odd Orchard near the cobwebbed tree, even though Beau assured them that the spiders posed no danger.

Beau informed them that they should not be too surprised if they ran into another group, which definitely piqued their interest, since that group would probably be the four girls. He also said he would attempt try to see them later in the evening.

When the four arrived at the dock, the water was tranquil. They waited patiently for any activity. Crow showed them the supply of squash kept to entice Sybil and explained to them how his dad discovered her penchant for her special fruit.

They all were becoming impatient, when Crow decided to try a different tactic.

He saw his father use it once and it worked in getting the serpent to respond. They went to the boathouse and got two elm paddles his dad would strike just above the water.

Crow started to bang away. It reverberated very loudly and brought a smile to Beau's face as he heard its distant echo.

It produced a look of amusement from Indigo, as she immediately realized it probably was her brother attempting to do what her dad succeeded in doing regularly. She asked the group if they were ready to move on to the dock to meet Sybil. Tara and Candice were animated with anticipation, since Indigo and Winter had discussed their encounter with Sybil. They left for Cryptic Bay.

Finally, on the horizon beyond the bay, the water started to stir. In the moonlight, a serpentine figure could be seen winding its way toward the dock. The Schnoggin' Knockers stood in awe as the great creature moved closer to the dock.

The four girls arrived at a small hillock above the dock. They, too, could now see the distinctly serpentine figure gracefully displacing water and rapidly closing to where the boys stood.

Indigo said, "Come on, let's join them."

Crow stood closest to the water, holding a squash in each hand with his arms extended. Sybil, with a distinguished look, elevated herself, towering over the four boys. Todd, Edgar and Larry watched with hypnotic wonderment as Crow comfortably presented the squash to Sybil, who immediately picked the one in his left hand and devoured it. The great serpent waited in anticipation for her next treat.

Crow offered, "Who wants to feed her next?"

Edgar immediately volunteered and did as Crow had, wincing slightly as the breath of Sybil struck his face, but mission accomplished, as he backed up to Todd and Larry. Crow retrieved two more squash from his basket for Todd and Larry to offer.

He was interrupted by Indigo's voice several yards in back of them, as she shouted, "I hope you have enough squash for us, too."

"You're kidding, you don't get any," Crow teased.

The three boys turned around and Crow continued, "Welcome to the party. We have plenty of squash." He began handing them out to everyone. Each, thrilled at the opportunity, in turn stepped forward to feed Sybil, who was unperturbed by the number of people who were participating in her personal feast. She had never eaten this much squash before and the permanently etched smile on her face seemed to grow larger.

When they had exhausted all the squash, the eight stood and watched her circle the bay and head out to sea. The thrill of the event was astonishing and each embraced the other in sheer joy. Todd hugged Indigo in delight. From his vantage point on the hillock from which the girls descended to the dock, Beau savored the moment too, because the entire day had been an unprecedented event in his extraordinary life. This filled him with hope about the condition, human condition, which now appeared less puzzling. He decided to join them in a few minutes, after they settled down.

A short time later he walked across the dock to where they were gathered and was greeted warmly by his new friends. After a bit, he asked them if he could express himself about the day. They sat down in front of him, Indigo with Inky in hand, as Beau got into what almost looked like a yoga position.

He began, "First of all, I want to thank you all for this remarkably amazing day. It's one I'll never forget. It was my privilege to be graced by your presence, because all of you are the best of your species. You represent hope for your conflicted world. The love you've expressed for each other here, represents the best quality of what it is to be human.

"Earlier this evening, I had a chance to talk to Larry, Edgar, Todd and Crow and they informed me of things I've observed about you. What I've studied mostly about you was focused on the darkness that often overtakes you. Yes, those are true circumstances within your species, but the one true thing about each of you is that, strangely, you suppress and hide your immense capacity to love. When you exercise it, you are sublimely beautiful."

He continued, "What intrigues me, is the unity you've evidenced tonight. There is not a more important part of your lives. It's as if you have all fallen into some kind of stupor about the collective joy you give each other. Clearly, you have awakened joy many times in your history. Reawaken it in your world of today. My advise to you is to stay as connected and alert as you are now, feed off these feelings, as if they were life-giving fauna. Let it grow into a hunger you 'demand' to be satisfied. Your capacity to love is your greatest gift."

Each of the eight looked at the others in their group with a different perspective. This was, indeed, an awakening and the group quickly returned to the feelings of joy they had experienced feeding Sybil. Inky was now the focus of attention of the boys, but the camaraderie was shared by everyone. Beau said farewell to each as he received their embrace. He departed, leaving them to their evening of discovery and happiness.

The next morning, Indigo woke at first dawn. She got up, stretched and smiled at Winter who was curled up with her Teddy bear in the other bed. She wanted to see the sunrise and enjoy the soft light of morning on M J Manor. She walked down the hall and decided to peek into Candice and Tara's room. At first she was startled to see that a bed was unoccupied, but was quickly relieved when she saw the two sleeping in the other bed. She smiled and moved down to the garden exit. Outside, she saw Frances and Betty working in the vegetable garden. She walked to them, "Good morning," and embraced each. She paced the estate grounds reveling in the enduring joy of the previous evening.

The Monsterjunkie household and invited guests assembled in the dining room for a breakfast buffet, the first and last event of the day. Talon and Pandora mingled with them, expressing their pleasure in meeting them. Indigo embraced both parents and thanked them profusely for this splendid opportunity.

For the guests, it ended all too soon as they filtered out of the manor to their respective rides—each contemplating the future with a stronger sense of hope. This marked the time when new paths were to be taken with the challenges and adventures that would inevitably present themselves along the way. They, however, had something new to rely on—each other.

❧ 26 ❧

Growing Conspiracy

Rutherford J Grimes III brooded over his embarrassment and temporary loss of power, wondering how quickly his father could resolve the situation with little Miss Winter. Even now he was fantasizing about ways to attack or disable all of the "deviant" types who populated the school, and especially the Monsterjunkie household. He felt certain he could marshal the forces necessary to expose M J Manor for what it really was, a freak show. He displayed a devious smile in anticipation of the undertaking.

Suddenly, the thought of elaborating the occurrence with Winter, to his father changed his demeanor, a furrow of concern crossed his brow. Rutherford was a handsome young man who never chose to exploit his talents, except two—his capacity to influence others around him and his skill in ducking the responsibility and consequences of his carefully conceived actions. He had a good physique he chose not to sculpt for athletics and was topped by thick brown hair drooping over his angular face. He carefully prepped himself for the meeting with his dad; he would simply convince him Winter's claims were exaggerated. Any harm inflicted on her was her own doing and certainly not from him or his friends. He strongly felt he could succeed with this explanation because she was in a category of people he knew his father disliked.

Ruth always cautiously contemplated every response his father could have to any and all things he communicated. He catered to his father's personal tastes—his views on economics, political beliefs and, most importantly, social status. He sensed his parents were preoccupied with how people perceived them, especially in the way they promoted the idea they were a family of wealth and position, the true central theme of their lives.

Mr. Rutherford Jameson Grimes II continued what his father, Ruth's grandfather, did in the world of investments. He was particularly successful in exploiting a mortgage industry that allowed unqualified people to make ill-advised home purchases. He covered himself very thoroughly, always deferring ultimate responsibility to others, thereby avoiding any legal entanglements for himself. Those answering for their misdeeds, simply deserved their fate because they didn't have the foresight to see the financial tsunami coming.

When the market imploded, he escaped scot free with even greater wealth than previously possessed, which, in part, was awarded to him by an inheritance from the original Grimes. His wife, Cynthia, insisted they have the biggest house in the most affluent neighborhood of Foggy Point and he happily agreed. Country club memberships and being invited to the most prestigious gatherings were aggressively pursued, although more than a few people in those groups viewed the two with near disdain. The refrain among those few was, "They try much too hard."

However, the political positions they embraced and the considerable money they contributed to those causes, allowed their perceived social climbing to be tolerated and they were allowed to enter those prestigious circles.

Rutherford thought it strange, that unlike his son, none of his associates ever addressed him as "Ruth," his shortened name, it was always the formal Rutherford. Not really worried about any close relationships, he simply dismissed the formality as an odd quirk of the people who greeted him, so he gave it no thought, despite the fact just about everyone around him had a nickname or an abbreviated version of their given name.

He sat in his study waiting for his son to arrive at their scheduled meeting and smiled with gratification when he heard a knock on his door at precisely 7:00, exactly the time he set for their scheduled meeting.

"Come in Ruth. I'm glad you're so prompt," he exclaimed with forced friendliness. "Before I forget, your mother sends her regards. She is planning to spend a few more days in New York, but will return in time for the party at the country club."

"Thanks, Dad, I really look forward to our meetings and please say hello to Mom for me," Ruth responded with careful formality. He asked, "May I sit down," as his father gestured to a small sitting area with two chairs.

They seated themselves, as Rutherford posed the question, "So, what really happened with that Winter girl? I'd like you to be candid with me, because some of what she says seems preposterous."

Ruth inhaled deeply and presented his carefully crafted lie, "You see, Dad, this girl, Winter, is one of the people we've talked about. I'm completely in step with what the family believes about social parasites, like her. She's one of those oddballs of society that lives off of the work of people like you. She's probably a little funny." Ruth carefully avoided the word 'gay,' since he knew his father disliked the word.

He continued, "Nick, Logan and I saw her sketching down by the lake, we just thought we'd take a look at what she was doing. The three of us aren't mean to people, we don't deliberately go around hurting people, I'd never do anything to embarrass the family. I know that would be an intolerable thing for you and Mom.

"So I asked politely if I could see her sketches, then suddenly, she turned very emotional and rude. She got up and dropped her sketchpad. I picked it up and started to glance at her drawings. There were some nature pictures and the oddest one of all was a sketch of two freakish giants. I tried to be funny and asked if those two were her relatives. That's when she became hysterical. I quickly showed Logan and Nick and they got a chuckle out of it, too. She grabbed the sketchpad and ran off. She was so clumsy and uncoordinated, she fell down a couple of times, that was the last we saw of her."

Rutherford relaxed somewhat and asked him, "Were you drinking before that happened? That's what they claimed in the police report."

Ruth, feigning complete indignation, exclaimed, "That's a complete lie. If you want to know what I think, I believe she made up this story to try to exploit us with some kind of trumped up charge to get money out of us, that's exactly what you've told me about how these social parasites operate. They try to bleed good honest citizens like you dry. I really hope you nip this in the bud as soon as possible."

Rutherford smiled with great satisfaction at his son's outburst and said, "Don't worry, our attorney is doing his job. Something interesting just occurred to me when you mentioned the sketch of those giants, there have been numerous rumors of people like that living in M J Manor. The place is one of the oddest in New England.

I've checked into the background of that family. Actually they're quite rich—old European money the family founder brought with him from Bavaria. They were actually quite influential in some circles. you know the scientific and environmental types, nobody we'd associate with. I know—What's his name? Oh yes, Talon—he is the heir to his father's fortune, who was well know around these parts for his philanthropy. I know he has an excellent attorney and clearly is a person to deal with carefully. He also teaches part time at Maine College. Do you suspect the Winter girl has any connections to that family?"

"Yes, I do. Those are the kind of people Winter Hodges would hang around with—tree hugging, artsy-fartsy types. In fact, I'd bet money that the girl who accompanied her to the police station was probably Indigo Monsterjunkie, a snooty intellectual who makes 'A's in every course she takes. She's probably an elitist feminist of some kind. It wouldn't surprise me if they were both dykes, disgusting."

Rutherford smiled, paused for a long time and then asked Ruth, "Why don't you start doing a little investigating yourself? See what you can find out about these people, but be very careful. You know what to do, let other people do the legwork and you collect the information. Let's see if you can turn up anything we can act on, OK?"

"Dad, I can't thank you enough for the vote of confidence you've given me. You are the best dad I could have. I'll get on it immediately and get back to you to discuss what I find." They shook hands and Ruth left the room with a satisfied smirk. He thought, *'Damn, I pulled it off. Now I get to go after all those creeps. I'll enlist Nick and he'll find the people to ask about them. I know they're hiding something there, I just know it.'*

Nick Stenson, a nervous, pimple-faced kid, was the only child of his twice-divorced father, an investment banker, who had little to no contact with his son, because much of the time he resided in Boston. Nick was also estranged from his mother, resulting from her unchecked alcoholism. He found some comfort from his stepmother, who was beginning to feel the pain of isolation from her husband because of his frequent trips to Boston and a growing suspicion that he was engaging in an extramarital affair. Seeking an identity or some connection in his confused world, he opted for friendship with Ruth, which, considering he saw no other real option, was not, in his mind, a bad choice.

Actually, he perceived it as a good situation. Ruth was generous with his largesse, mostly quality alcohol, superior weed and occasional money, and the dubious feeling that he enjoyed a comfortable status connection with Ruth. After all, both his father and Ruth's were roughly in the same profession.

When Ruth called on him to do something, "really important," he responded immediately. They met on a quiet little veranda on an unobserved part of Ruth's sprawling house. Ruth arrived at their sitting area with a six-pack of cold beer and two joints of very "exotic" weed. They partook of a couple brews and then lit up.

Ruth explained what he wanted Nick to do, "Listen, I've got the green light from Dad to do some investigation on the Monsterjunkie crowd. I know they are supporting Winter in that stupid a–s police complaint she filed against us. By the way, my dad's lawyer will stop that dead in its tracks. They simply have no 'real' evidence. Now, it's time for us to go on the offensive against the very people who are involved with this, which are the same deviants and creeps that are messing up our society."

Nick asked, "What can we do?"

"Let's learn some more things about M J Manor and get all the dirt on the Monsterjunkies. See if you can talk to somebody who goes there regularly to get a feel for what the place is all about. You might start with someone who makes deliveries there—somebody like that, or maybe someone who does repair or service work.

My dad is doing some follow-ups from his sources. He's even hiring people in Europe to find out stuff about them there. They're very rich; that we know, but we both suspect they're up to no good, especially with people like Winter Hodges as their friends. I especially want to pin something on that creep, Crow Monsterjunkie, and some of his friends, too."

Nick and Logan, who had been absent from school on the day of the tampon incident on the playground, heard the rumor of what happened from others who circulated the story, often with conflicting facts about what really went down. They both thought it prudent to keep their mouths shut about it and only discuss it, if Ruth brought it up—which he seemed to have no intention of doing. Ruth brooded over it and fantasized about revenge, which now, more than ever, seemed like a real possibility. Nick now sensed Ruth's eagerness to exact pain on those who humiliated him, especially Crow.

Nick mentioned, "I'll go to their delivery guy first and see what he has to say. He's got to know something about the place. I'll let you know what's up as soon as I can."

∞ 27 ∞

The Delivery

Before school the next morning, Nick sought out Ruth at their usual meeting place and the two walked to school together. Nick said, "I think I've learned something important about M J Manor. I located a delivery guy who spilled his guts to me. I slipped him a twenty to get him talking, and he confessed he takes a lot of very weird animals to the manor. I learned from somebody else that he's the only one who takes anything to their estate. I get the feeling they are dealing with some pretty dangerous stuff, I wouldn't be surprised if some of it's illegal."

Ruth smiled and said, "Very good, that's precisely the kind of information I want. Here let me pay you back for that twenty you passed him."

Nick said, "There's really no need to . . ."

Ruth pulled a hundred dollar bill from his wallet and stuffed it into his hand, "Take this, you've really earned it. No arguments."

"Well, I guess, sure."

They arrived at school early, where they planned to meet Logan to bring him into their conspiracy. Talking in front of their locker, they both briefed Logan, a tall, skinny blonde kid, on finding all kinds of information they needed. As traffic in the hallway began to increase, they were about to conclude their meeting when Ruth opened his locker and was greeted by a small avalanche of tampons that fell all around him on the floor. He stood there gaping in disbelief, as a chorus of giggles began to echo throughout the hallway.

Someone they couldn't identify at the other end of the hallway shouted, "Oh no, Ruthy baby."

Ruth contained his rage, as Nick and Logan helped him throw the tampons into a nearby trashcan. He hissed, "Find out who did this. Let me tell you, they're gonna' pay for this. Let's get to class. You guys know what to do."

That evening, Ruth knew he would say nothing of the school incident, to admit to being humiliated would appear weak in his father's estimation, but nevertheless, patiently waited for an audience with his father. He was chomping at the bit to pass along Nick's information and secretly fuming inside about the prank.

He recently learned there were more than just Logan, Nick, and himself, who felt as they did about the "wrong" types beginning to populate the area. Logan got on board with the program and did some serious canvassing of the like-minded. Ruth suspected they were a small group within the population along the coast of Maine, but it was clear to him he needed more allies. How could he marshal those people to support the views of the only really sane minority— the people who agreed with Dad and him?

He knocked on the door at exactly 7:00 pm and not a minute sooner or later. He knew that punctuality was an important expectation and he was adept at pushing his dad's buttons to get favorable responses to his requests.

"Come in, Ruth," he heard from the other side, "I've been expecting you."

He entered the room and immediately noticed the sitting table where they usually sat had a bottle of cognac and two cigars and two glasses. His dad rose and shook hands with him.

"Have a seat, Ruth. We have a lot of things to cover and I thought it was time you experienced one of life's great pleasures, cognac and a good cigar."

Ruth, feigning surprise, said, "Dad, I'm so honored you'd do this for me, I can't thank you enough. I'd like to try the cigar later if you don't mind. I'm not sure I could handle one of your Havana cigars."

"Sure, son. Let me pour some cognac," as he sloshed a healthy portion of rare XO into the two crystalline snifters and carefully, with pride, lit up a cigar for himself.

Ruth lifted his glass and tipped his father's, "Here's to you, Dad."

"Here's to us," replied Rutherford Jameson Grimes II.

After a while, Ruth couldn't resist watching his dad smoke his cigar. He was captured by it. Looking at his dad, he seemed like an imperious, take-control captain of industry—and, at that moment, he wanted to bask in the same light of such a personage.

He decided to temporarily duck out of his hypocritical façade and ask to smoke a stogie with him.

He asked, " Dad, looking at you, I think I'm ready to try that cigar. Can you show me how to light it?"

"Very good. Remember not to inhale. I know you don't smoke, so just don't take the smoke into your lungs. This is a taste experience, not a nicotine rush. See those thin cedar strips on the tray there? They are called cedar spills, Spanish cedar, that gives a very nice burn on the foot of the cigar. First you cut off the head of the cigar with one of these bullet punch cutters. Here we go. I'll do it for you." After cutting the end of the cigar, he handed it to Ruth.

"Thanks Dad, this is great."

"Go ahead and light the cedar spills. You don't want, if you can help it, to light a cigar with a match because the sulfur will contaminate the tobacco. Be sure you light up the whole foot. Go ahead and light her up."

Ruth feigned clumsiness but after two attempts, he was blowing smoke. He watched his dad smoke and made sure he imitated him. He sipped some cognac, drew on the cigar and slowly exhaled the smoke.

He shared, "I think I know why you like these, especially with the taste of cognac in your mouth. Thanks for this today, this is a special moment for me. If you don't mind, I'd like to tell you about what I've learned."

"Go ahead, I have quite a bit to run by you, but I'd like to hear from you first."

Ruth swallowed some cognac, took another drag off of his cigar and began, "I sent Nick over to the local delivery service and he pushed the M J Manor delivery guy hard for information. He also bribed him with twenty bucks. To quote Nick, 'He spilled his guts.' It looks like they really do have a lot of strange animals and a lot of them are pretty spooky and dangerous.

"He found out they have only one delivery person go to that address, because all of the others don't want to get near the place. I thought that was powerful information and knew you'd want to know immediately. And, I reimbursed him with a hundred, which he tried to decline. I hope I did the right thing. He took some serious risks doing that."

"You did the right thing. That information is worth a lot more than a Ben Franklin. Actually, you deserve compensation for setting this up. I'm going to beef up your allowance this week." He pulled out $300 in paper bills he passed over to him.

"Thanks Dad, you don't have to do this… you're the most generous person I know."

Rutherford II settled into his chair and took another drag off his cigar and confidently spoke, "I've had our lawyer hire some investigators and they've turned up some fascinating information. I don't know how much it will help us yet, but it has certainly aroused a lot of suspicion in me.

Talon Monsterjunkie's close friend in Romania, in Transylvania no less, is a nobleman, who is a descendent of one of their historic rulers centuries ago, his name is Alexandru Anescu. They both have very similar interests and often cooperate on expeditions to remote lands, where they've found some of these dangerous animals. He owns an estate near the Carpathian Mountains, which is pretty much operating the same way Monsterjunkie manages his place.

Our lawyer's agent interviewed several people in a small community in the region near the Anescu Estate and learned quite a bit. Apparently, both of them are Freemasons and they attend their lodges with some regularity. When I heard this, I immediately flashed on the potential connection of the Monsterjunkie family to the Illuminati, which began in Bavaria. It actually gave me chills. If we confirm this, we must proceed with the utmost caution. These are, supposedly, very dangerous people.

Ruth, who postured as being intensely interested, asked, "Dad, I don't know much about this group, what's the story on them?"

"I'm no authority either, but I've heard some people at the club say they are very powerful and they are pulling the strings behind a lot of the things that are going on politically. I honestly don't know if that's true or a lot of BS. I'd need a lot more evidence to support that idea to be convinced. I know some executives in the financial world who say it's too complex for any one group to figure out, much less control. If you look at their supposed history, when the original group started, they enlisted some of the most talented people of their time. That's neither here nor there, what's important is the here and now."

"You're right, Dad. At the end of the day, it's all about the problem of this Monsterjunkie family, their oddball friends and how they're trying to change the community we love by flooding it with undesirables. What should we do?"

"Do as I'm doing now, which is enlisting people who think like us. We can actually be very strong without being terribly big. Let's continue to investigate these people and then, when the time is right, we'll expose them for what they are and place them where they belong—either powerless, or out of the States."

"Dad, you'll be happy to know that I've taken those first steps. Nick and Logan are recruiting people, as we speak."

"Excellent, I'm very proud of how you've handled this. Let's stay the course, then maybe down the road we can say, 'mission accomplished.'"

They tipped their brandy snifters and drew on their cigars with the satisfaction that they were the true saviors of the American way.

∞ 28 ∞

Two Thank Yous

Todd Fielding, the first to declare the establishment of the Schnoggin' Knockers, was puzzled over a couple of thank you notes he would place in the two flower arrangements he intended to send to M J Manor. His mother suggested the idea, since it was so obvious he had such a wonderful time staying there. Besides, a big motivation for Todd to do this was that his mother agreed to pay for both arrangements.

To his parents, Todd was quite careful not to elaborate those parts of the experience that involved Beau, or anything that would compromise M J Manor. He carefully skirted the edges of any discussion of animals and never made any reference to the two giants, Betty and Frances. Todd's assessment of the ball was mostly focused on the young people who attended, especially Indigo Monsterjunkie.

Sending a floral arrangement and thank you note to Pandora was an easy exercise and simple courtesy. However, the one he was to send to Indigo caused him some consternation because he ached to know her better and wanted to ask her out on a date. His reservations were twofold. Besides the obvious one that he could simply be rejected, was that he was two years younger than Indigo, which could be a possible impediment and he knew, if she agreed to go out with him, she might press him to tell more about the Schnoggin' Knockers. He eventually decided that all of those reasons were completely bogus and went ahead and asked her out on the thank you card.

When he finally purchased the flowers, included the appropriate cards in each arrangement and had everything packaged, he confidently marched off with them to the town's delivery office to have them forwarded to M J Manor. When he arrived at the office, a short distance away, he was surprised to see Nick at the loading area talking to Reggie, the deliveryman, of whom Todd knew through Crow's funny stories about him.

His instincts told him to observe the scene from a safe and unobserved distance behind a large truck parked on the street; thereby, keeping his presence unknown to Nick. Todd loved being a detached observer of the human condition, especially if it was observing people he disliked. When he saw Nick, after a short time, leave the area, he decided to approach Reggie to ask him about the improbable contact with Nick.

When Nick left, he went directly to Reggie and introduced himself. He said, "Pardon me, sir, my name is Todd Fielding and I'm a friend of Crow Monsterjunkie. I know of you through Crow, who really admires your work for his father. Was the kid talking to you, asking about M J Manor?"

"As a matter of fact, he tried to press me on it. We don't disclose our contacts with our clients and anything one could say about M J Manor is usually about the strangeness of the place. We don't say much about their estate, but I did let it slip that some unusual animals live there."

"Did you sense he was satisfied with your answer?"

"Yea, we didn't talk long. There was something irritating about him, I think he was about to bribe me for some so-called inside stuff. Do you know this guy? He had a smug, superior air about him."

"Sir, if you'll forgive my bluntness, I think Nick is a complete a—hole. However, I'm a good friend of Crow's and, I can assure you, there's nothing to fear from M J Manor. I would love to expand on that, but that's all I can say. Thank you for your time. By the way, I need to have these two arrangements delivered to the very same address, and I'd appreciate it, if you'd take special care. Have a great day."

Reggie smiled at him slightly amused by his style and just a little bit relieved about his comment on the safety of M J Manor. He asked, "Do you know anything about the mailbox?"

"Sorry sir, I can't help you there."

When he got home, he called Crow immediately to explain what happened, and suggested that the four get together ASAP.

They met in the park that afternoon. Todd said to Crow, "Your delivery guy didn't give Nick much, other than there are some really exotic creatures living on your grounds. Reggie described Nick as 'irritating,' 'smug', and having a 'superior air,' which, considering who he hangs with, is almost a compliment. You can be sure that Ruthy talked him into pushing Reggie about your place. Do you have any idea what's going on?"

"Actually I do, I listened to my father speak with one of his European friends on the phone. He invited me to do that, which was the first time ever for me. He was talking through Skype to Romania, which he and his friend regularly use. When my great grandfather moved to America, he gave all of his animals to a Romanian family,

169

and their ancestors have been our friends ever since. You're not going to believe where they live. It's in Transylvania."

Larry interjected, " Wow. That's where Dracula lived. That's awesome. What do they say about the legends?"

Edgar said, "Hey, I've studied that legend in history class. A ruler of the time was a dude by the name of Vlad Tepes. It was in his family the name Count Dracula got started. They called him the 'Impaler.' He used to put his enemies on stakes just like the insects we see on pins in biology lab. I guess he did that to hundreds of people. He was one nasty dude."

Crow continued, "You got that right, but, strangely enough, his descendents, who are my father's friends, are some of the coolest people in Europe. They have an incredible estate in Transylvania, which is a big chunk of Romania. I'll show you some pictures the next time you guys are over. It's at the base of the Carpathian Mountains and they have two or three times the acreage we do here. They collect exotic animals just like my father."

"So what did they tell your dad?" asked Todd.

"His friend in Transylvania—his name is Alexandru Anescu—could be my father's twin; they even have done animal adventures together. But, anyway, they both have really good security. If someone is making a lot of inquiries about either one of them, they usually know about it quickly. What he told my father was, someone from our community was asking a lot of questions about us—and them.

"They, or maybe their agents, were snooping around in a lot of different places. They probably contacted people in towns near their estate. There are a lot of so-called 'monster' legends about their place, just like ours. In that part of the world, there are a lot of people who believe in monsters, in some cases for good reasons. We're really not sure what they've learned."

Larry asked, "What kind of animals do they keep? Do they have intelligent beings like Beau?"

"Not that I know of, but it wouldn't surprise me if they did, I know they have some of the same kinds of birds we do and they have a big cloning lab that's working with ancient eggshells to recreate extinct birds. We have one here, Peepers, the Dodo bird."

"What about the scary stuff from movies, you know, the vampire bat legends associated with Dracula?" asked Edgar. "I heard they were real."

"They have a complete colony and they feed on the only thing they can really eat, mammal blood. Hold on, before you wig out, it's all a controlled experiment to find and use an enzyme the bats produce when they drink blood. It thins out the blood so the bats can slurp it up better. They extract the blood from cattle and put it in dishes and the bats drink away. They want to use the enzyme to help stroke victims to dissolve blood clots. My father says they are actually using this in Sweden and they'll eventually be using it in Romania."

Todd added, "I'm sure, if the people in town knew they had that colony, they'd start screaming 'monsters.' There'd be torch carrying mobs ready to burn the place down."

"I'm not sure, but just saying 'vampire bat,' freaks most people out. Most of their contacts are with farm animals or jungle mammals and they only take a superficial amount of blood. But let's get back to the immediate problem, the Grimes family and their friends—a special 'breed' of vampire. I'm sure they're the ones behind all of this. We need a plan," Crow explained.

Crow emphasized, "It's clear to me they are trying to dig up something on my family. I'm sure Ruthy despises me with a passion, so he's trying to figure out a way to hurt me, or indirectly, hurt my family. At this point, we really don't know what he's up to, so I think the best thing we can do is gather some info and then act on that."

Todd added, "We'll ask the people we know to help us. Nick will probably tell somebody else, or someone else will overhear him. What's the name of the other dick with ears—Oh yeah—Logan Crenshaw. I'll get a friend of mine who knows him, to see if he can get anything out of him, without being too obvious about it.

Larry asserted, "We'll do the same and it's probably a good idea if we tell Candice, Indigo, Winter, and Tara. What do you think?"

"You're right. I'll call Indigo and she'll tell the others," Crow said.

Edgar agreed, "Looks like we're all on the same page. OK, now it's time for the Schnoggin' Knocker salute." He paused and said, "Do you think we should grab our balls on this one?"

Larry responded, "Probably not, there are too many people around, so let's skip that part."

Todd seconded him, "People would probably think it's weird, they'd think we have something wrong with our plumbing."

The four raised their fists and shouted without any other gestures, "Schnoggin' Knockers. Schnoggin' Knockers. Schnoggin' Knockers."

Larry and Edgar left and Todd immediately turned to Crow and confided in him, saying, "Listen, my man, thanks to my mom, I've sent two flower arrangements to your mom and sister, I just wanted to let you know. I asked your sister out. I've enclosed a note on the card with the flowers, had to do it, I only hope she's just slightly interested."

Crow smiled at him and said, "You poor, love-sick dick-head. I'll check to see how she handles it, but I know my mother will like the flowers. Thanks, brother."

∞

Reggie pulled into the M J Manor driveway and stopped in front of Fang, the telepathic, mailbox with tentacles. Fang opened his mouth but telepathically said, "Good morning, Reggie. How are you this fine day?"

Somewhat surprised at the cordiality of the greeting, he replied, "It's going well and, by the way, thanks for calling me by my real name."

"No effort, the Monsterjunkies are enjoying a newly found informality and I'm merely getting in step with the program. I see you're carrying two flower arrangements, very nice, and another animal for Master Talon?"

"The last one I brought here I called 'scratchy,' and I call this one 'windy.' It keeps blowing. I don't know if it's inhaling or exhaling. Very weird, but that's par for the course here."

"And for me?" asked Fang.

"Just a couple of letters, one from Romania."

Reggie handed them to the tentacle that came out of the mailbox. The mailbox closed and Reggie pressed the service entrance button with a somewhat different feeling about the place. He pulled in front of the loading dock, where he greeted Dr. Monsterjunkie, who returned the greeting. Reggie said, "Good morning, sir."

"Good morning to you, Reggie." Reggie smiled at the new form of address.

173

Talon gushed over the floral gifts and said, "Pandora and Indigo will be pleased to receive these exquisite arrangements. Now Reggie, if you don't mind, help me open this crate. I've been waiting so long for this shipment."

Talon, and Reggie, with less trepidation than the last time, began to pry open the ventilated top of the crate. When they finally removed the lid, what they saw was the spines of a creature that could only can be described as a living balloon.

"Reggie, this is an inflatable Mongolian hedgehog."

"If you say so, sir."

Talon, with excitement, said, "I'll pull him from the crate so we can see his face. Here we go." Wearing leather gloves, he held up the hedgehog, which was now the size of a beach ball, where both of them could see its face. He continued, "This represents a remarkable adaptation, Reggie. There are more than a few creatures that can change shape or color very quickly, such as chameleons, mimic octopi, and puffer fish to name a few. Let's put him on the dock and see if he deflates."

Reggie asked, "Sir, do you think he puffs up when something unknown threatens him?"

"Let's test your hypothesis," as Talon advanced to the Mongolian mini-giant that had now deflated. "Sure enough Reggie, he's starting to balloon up again. Oh my goodness. He's rolling down the dock. Go around to where he is and catch him, please."

Reggie dashed to the end of the dock and caught him, as he was about to go over the edge. He grimaced when the hedgehog passed some serious wind.

Talon rushed up to them and declared, "This little guy will take awhile to adapt to his new environment, but eventually he'll be all right."

Reggie asked, "Sir, may I ask, what drives you to find animals like these? That's got to be very hard work."

Talon smiled and said, "It's a long story, Reggie, but I learned a lot of it from my father. He loved all life, animal or human. I guess our family's attraction to the hidden creatures of the world, is a combination of passionate curiosity, plus traveling to the many obscure places we have to go to find them. We also have strong allies in our pursuits, who enjoy the same passion. Honestly, sometimes I don't know who finds whom, our encounters go beyond what one would consider normal coincidence. There is certainly a kind of mutual attraction that kicks in, I can't explain it, it's simply a part of me."

Reggie thoughtfully reflected and said, "My momma used to say that all good things start with the love of life. It seems you're living out that saying."

"Your mother's wise. Thanks for seeing that in me."

Talon removed his gloves and they shook hands and said their goodbyes. As Reggie drove off the grounds, he felt a strange bonding with M J Manor, one that he had never even remotely conceived of feeling when he began his duties here. He thought to himself, '*If I start enjoying this, people will begin to change their attitudes about this place. I think I'll just frown when somebody asks me about M J Manor and keep my mouth shut. Oh yeah, I will allow those folks to continue to buy me food and drink at our pub. After all, it wouldn't be right to break a tradition. But there's still that crazy damn mailbox.*' He smiled happily as he continued his delivery route.

∞ 29 ∞

A Dinner Invitation

Indigo sat in her room fixed on two recent events, Winter's phone call to her and her brother Crow's recent warning regarding Ruth's friends snooping around about M J Manor. Winter confided in her that the police complaint had been dismissed, something Indigo had intuitively felt would happen; nevertheless, she still had hoped for a successful prosecution. Indigo reassured Winter that she now had seven friends that would be looking out for her and it would be highly unlikely that Ruth's group could ever repeat such an act.

That outsiders were now trying to place M J Manor under some kind of investigative microscope, she found genuinely disconcerting. She had always hoped she could create a social climate and still preserve the manor's uniqueness and somewhat private nature without seriously compromising it and felt she had succeeded beyond expectations; but, now, an actual threat was afoot. *Was it because of her legal support of Winter or was it just an inevitable result of the forces involved in the potential conflict?* She was starting to weigh in favor of the latter explanation.

Her thoughts were interrupted by a knock on the door and Pandora's request to come in. Pandora smiled, "I have a lovely surprise for you," as she entered the room with the flower arrangement Todd sent her.

"Oh Mother, it's beautiful. Who's it from?"

"It's from Todd Fielding."

Indigo laughed and said, "He's such a romantic and was so much fun at our party."

"He sent one to me, too. What a nice gesture. Tell me, do you like him?" queried Pandora.

"Well, yes, I guess I do. I like all of Crow's new friends and aren't you amazed at how Crow has changed? He's growing up. He seems so focused and he's finally acknowledged how smart he really is," said Indigo.

"I understand what you mean, I think he has grown closer to his father. Your father has a new energy about him, as well. I think our social gathering was a great success, but we still need to be cautious. He talked to Alexandru Anescu recently and someone from our community was attempting to gather information on both our families."

Indigo added, "I was about to tell you the same thing. Crow texted to say Grimes and his sleazy friends are probably behind it. Those types are around here now and they seem to be asserting themselves more and more. I think we need to be watchful, but just like father would say, 'Don't let fear drive our actions.' Mother, do you have any idea when we'll go back to Europe again? I'd love to see Bavaria and visit Alexandru in Romania. Crow and I were so young the last time we went, we barely remember what it was like."

Pandora smiled and mused on the possibility, "What a lovely thought, I'll start to plant those seeds in Talon's fertile mind. Interesting, how would you feel about taking your friends along?"

"Mother, what an awesome idea. Of course, I'd love to. What an adventure and I'm sure Crow would want to do the same."

"Oh, Indy, I almost forgot. Apparently, Todd got the thank you messages mixed up. Here's his card and a note attached with a request to go out to dinner. How do you feel about that?"

"I like him, but I'm not sure I'd date him, although he could be a lot of fun, I guess. It's a little strange going out with one of Crow's friends, but I might be open to the idea. I'll think about it. But lets get back to our immediate problems with our family and friends. How should we deal with the people who obviously want to hurt us?"

Pandora paused and finally said, "We'll go tit for tat, if they want to get something on us, we'll get something on them. I'll talk to Talon about having our attorney hire some investigators to pursue this. After all, isn't the Grimes family a bunch of *nouveau riche poseurs*, who have a very dubious history of business and financial dealings? It should be relatively easy to crack open their phony façade. I know they can snoop around forever about us, or the Anescu family, and only pick up fragments of information and rumors.

"The Munsterjung family, just like the Anescu family, is old Europe and knows how to survive crises. After all, both are now prospering after the most horrendous wars in history. Trust me, we'll figure this out, Indy, and in the mean time, just be alert, and more important than anything else, love and care for your friends. That is what really matters. OK or 'va bene' "

Indigo embraced her mother and said, "Thank you, Mother. You're wonderful. You know, I'm going to accept Todd's offer for dinner, just for the fun of it and, perhaps, learn a little bit more about brother and his friends."

"Good, that should be fun. Just remember one important thing; he's probably in love with you." Pandora smiled and noted Indy's surprised look at the statement.

❧ 30 ❧

Pictures

Tara Caruso left the weekly meeting of the New England Gay and Lesbian Alliance with only slightly less confusion than before she walked into the group's gathering to see what their life style was all about. The warmth of her recollections of the Monster's Ball weekend moderated her confusion, as she walked away from the restaurant's large meeting room where the gathering was held.

The concluding evening episode of that wonderful day was the source of her confusion. When she and Candice returned to their room in M J Manor, they were fatigued but still very much filled with excitement. They readied themselves for bed, looked at each other, laughed, and then embraced. Candice kissed her deeply and the extended embrace felt very good to her. They slept together and genuinely savored the physical connection they enjoyed. They kissed briefly, stroked each other without intimate touching and fell asleep.

Tara awakened first, dressed and left to look for Indigo in the manor gardens, while Candice slept until later in the morning. At the brunch, which brought to a close their weekend adventure, there was no change in either girl's demeanor. They embraced each other just as everyone else did and departed for their respective homes.

As the days moved on, Tara began to assess the incident with greater scrutiny and she sought to understand her true feelings about her sexuality. She knew she liked some boys, but she also considered the fact that some of them were genuinely gay. She decided to check this group out, mostly to try to clarify her own mixed emotions. It helped her understand the people attending, but did not give her a clear impression of her own status.

As she left the restaurant, unbeknownst to her, she was being videoed from a hidden location across the street. Logan Crenshaw had his high def. video recording the entrance and exit of each individual who had attended the meeting. Before that, he took a shot of the placard at the entrance of the restaurant that announced the gay and lesbian gathering. He practically shouted for joy, when he recognized Tara among the people coming and going. He was thrilled to see her wish several people goodbye and hug them before they parted company, all captured on his camera.

He thought, *Ruth and Nick will flip, when they see this.* This is tailor made for exposing the fact that people on our campus are involved in these weird lifestyles. I'm just sorry that crazy Hodges girl wasn't here. That would have been perfect. Oh well, maybe next time.

A short time later, he joined Ruth and Nick on the veranda of the Grimes estate. They had agreed to discuss their plans. Both of Ruth's parents were out of town and no one would disturb the planning of their conspiracy and the alcohol and weed they intended to enjoy.

Ruth and his cronies decided they needed to be more aggressive in their condemnation of the 'outsiders' and decided to video those people in compromising situations. They were elated with Logan's work and proceeded to get drunk celebrating his triumph.

The next day, Tara discovered a series of pictures of her leaving the NEGLA meeting posted on her Facebook page. She had never been particularly careful about who she let be her friend and most of her friends managed their Facebook pages as she did, respectfully. She called Candice immediately and, unsurprisingly, she had gotten the same series of pictures. The pictures also contained salacious comments and disparaging slams against those in attendance.

It shocked then saddened her someone would go to the trouble of doing something so mean spirited; it dawned on her where something like this would come from. She flashed on Indigo's warning that Grimes and his crew were up to no good. They needed to talk and agreed to meet after school to sort this out.

∞ 31 ∞

What's Ahead?

T he Schnoggin' Knockers got together in the park after school to talk about their day. Larry said, "Did you see what Ruth was wearing today?" Todd replied, "Yeah, those gangsta duds?" They all laughed about Ruth's gangstahood and, as a group, raised their fists to chant, "Schnoggin' Knockers, Schnoggin' Knockers, Schnoggin' Knockers."

On a more serious note, Crow shared his feelings, "Honestly, I used to hate the manor and the animals. Nobody else had animals like that. I thought my family was weird and you guys were scared of us. But now I think the animals and you are incredible."

"Most people would love to have a place like yours," said Todd.

"As for the Monsterjunkie name, I've never liked being a Monsterjunkie. Think about it—Cromwell Monsterjunkie. Now I realize the name is dignified, a bit of flare, maybe even. But as for Cromwell, you know I don't like Cromwell. What am I, a British Lord or something?" Crow asked.

"You could be a British Lord, if you choose," replied Edgar.

"Nah, you know what I mean," said Crow. "It's the heritage of the Munsterjung family, the Munsterjung family name. What does it represent? What has the family accomplished? What is our future?

"The Monsterjunkie legacy is already established. Conrad, my great grandfather, was a visionary. And Ernest, my grandfather, upheld the Monsterjunkie name. Now my father, Talon, is a noted cryptozoologist, discovering new and unusual animals. Where do I fit? What's next for me?"

About the Author

Erik Daniel Shein was born Erik Daniel Stoops, November 18th 1966. He is an American writer, motion picture producer, screenwriter, voice actor, animator, entrepreneur, entertainer, philanthropist, Pet enthusiast and animal health advocate .

He is the author and co-author of over 30 nonfiction and fiction books whose writings include six scientific articles in the field of herpetology.

L. M. Reker is a college professor of English, at Glendale community college and graduate of Arizona state university. He has been married for 42 years, and has three natural sons and three sons, who for all practical purposes, are adopted. One being Erik Daniel Shein. He loves good writing researching and teaching.